FC...
THE MANY
NOT
THE FEW

VOLUME 32

ISBN: 9798865818724

All Rights Reserved
Named authors and contributors ©2023
Front Cover "Two Fingers To Poverty"
Art work front cover Meek ©2023

The authors have asserted their moral rights

An Inherit The Earth ©2023

Published by Amazon ©2023

Edited by CT Meek

First published 2023

[Dictum est numquam facere lucrum]

Authors:

Janette Fenton

Mark Ingram

Meek

Susan Broadfoot

Ian OPG London

Wendy Webb

Denny Paul Mills

Des Lane

John Mcmahon

George Colkitto

Steven Joseph McCrystal

David Norris-Kay

Jon Bickley

Michelle Carr

Robyn Isobel Florence McEwan

Patricia Bell

Giancarlo Moruzzi

Lawrence Reed

Celine Rose Mariotti

Niamh Mahon

Richard Earls

Contents -
The Mutual Appreciation Society
All I See Is Space
Soft and Sensual They Kissed the Sun
I Had A. . . Dream
England's Glory
I Chose To Wear Twigs
At That Moment
Penned This Morning
I Guess
If Your High Takes Control
Rush Hour @ The Hospital
Dame Villanelle
Disabled Toilet
I Should 'Ave Looked After Me Teeth 19 -34.
And I Must Go
Passing Time On A Spring
The Hours Are Passing Fast
Extracting The
Earning A Gold Star Along The Road
Whitby (Villanelle)
Spring Forward (Villanelle)
Selection Of Limericks
Holidays Are Hellish
Fortitude
Cirrhosis Of The Heart
Tension
On The Level
After A Good Day For Ice Cream
The Make Do Man
The Poet and The Circus Strongman

This Is The Land
Walk By The River
Anonymous
Our Rainbow Shone In Autumn Winds
Wound Up
On Swithering Heights (choosing between Roast Beef and Tongue at Morrisons)
Till The Curtain Drops
In Sand
Parallel Universe
Jimmy, Can Ye Spare A Rhyme
Flowers For The Girl
Moonbeams And Daydreams
The Chase Hurdles
Dragonflies
Exit
Ecology
Sun Song
Autumn Clouds
Self
Sixty
The Leaves Are Still Green
Waiting For Spring
Goodbye, Jazzy Cat
Alan
Burbage
The Monday Club
Silent Chaos
My Heart
Light
Double Take

Fall Is Falling
Red Jacket
Looking Back At Me
Betrayal
Gentle Man
Ode To Man
Circus
Holy Flame
Willow
Desperate Hours
The Warrior
Fate Foretold
Push The Plough
My Body's A Temple Part 1: Pills
Excerpt 10 from the epic poem The Barricade
Excerpt 11 from the epic poem The Barricade
If Not, Then Why Not?
A Weary World
Faces Of Yesteryear
A Musical Bear
Somewhere Long, Long Ago
Skinny, I Miss You
My Cup Overfloweth
Putting The Laundry Away
The Little Things
Mouse
Catalonian Roadside Poppies
Your Halo's Slipping
Bullies

The Mutual Appreciation Society

Like for like, meet kindred spirits the fly poster read. I'd also seen it stuck onto lamp posts, beneath street lights, and the occasional wall. Like For Like, come join the Mutual Appreciation Society. I must admit that it piqued my interest. I'd heard of mutual attraction, and mutual agreement, and I'd also heard faint whispers about mutual assured destruction (MAD), but that doctrine applied mainly to military and not your common passer-by. I had no intention of going nuclear with anyone, thank you very much.

I thought I may as well take up the offer of a free complimentary drink, alcoholic and non-alcoholic available, but not cordials. I liked that they didn't discriminate against alcoholism and teetotalism. If indeed it was and they and not just some sad random trying to entrap a vulnerable individual.

The meeting was arranged to be held in a church hall, a freezing cold church hall, a soulless church hall, used on Wednesdays for Karate and Thursdays for senile bingo. Occasionally it may be let for the odd birthday party or a hastily thrown together anniversary soiree, as an afterthought. Or so I'm led to believe. You decide.

Upon entering the venue I noticed that there was one fold away wooden table with an ornamental cover on it, set up with two plastic seats placed either side of it in the faraway left-hand side corner, dimly lit I may add. It was neither an intimate or alluring setting. On the table on a place mat there sat a half empty bottle of cheap supermarket own brand Rosé and a bowl of half-eaten assorted nibbles, which were mainly peanuts. It looked uninviting. One seat was empty and in the other a person sat holding a vanity mirror in front of him. Not full length, but not half-length either, somewhere in between. It had miniature LED lights around it. So I naturally sat down on the vacant seat. What ensues is a true account. Waivers and non-disclosures have been signed by all parties.

And so it began . . .

Other Person: Hello. Pleased to me you.
Me: Likewise, I'm sure.
Other Person: Do you have a name?
Me: Yes.
Other Person: What is it you do?
Me: I attend hastily arranged Mutual Appreciation meetings.
Other Person: Do you work? Are you in gainful employment?
Me: I wouldn't say gainful. More like in a voluntary capacity. I'm told I'm not wealthy but the rewards are immense, and that it'll look good on any future CVs that I may invent. Potential employers should be impressed.
Other Person: Do you have any common interests?
Me: Yes.
Other Person: For example what?
Me: I can speak. I'm human. I have feelings.
Other Person: Are you married?
Me: I used to be. I may still be.
Other Person: Are you single?
Me: I used to be. I think I still am.
Other Person: Do you follow politics?
Me: I did but lost the stamina to pursue them any further.

Other Person: Are you enthusiastic?
Me: Up to a point.
Other Person: Which point?
Me: To the point where I need a compass.
Other Person: Are you religious?
Me: I'm a devout atheist when I'm not brainwashed and bombarded with cultish, organised religion. I thought there was, is only one God to begin with. I'd say I'm more gregarious than religious.
Other Person: Have you ever suffered from depression?
Me: Even in my darkest, foulest, lowest mood I couldn't possibly comment. Depression is subjective: in my book.
Other Person: Do you play any sports?
Me: Tiddlywinks, dominoes, and the occasional game of mixed shinty. Papier-mâché keeps me busy.
Other Person: Do you have any other interests?
Me: Other than what?
Other Person: Oh, I'm afraid you're not permitted to answer a question with a question. I'll have to ask you to leave.
Me: Oh. Goodbye then.
Other Person: Goodbye. It was nice meeting you.
Me: Likewise.

So I switched off the LED lights and packed them away safely with my vanity mirror and departed. It's so nice to meet like-minded people, similar outliers, even momentarily. I left the wine, table and seats as they were. I often wonder how the other person's life turned out.

Meek

All I See Is Space

Read between the lines they said
It stares you in the face
Well, I've looked so hard I'm going blind
For all I see is space.

Janette Fenton

Soft And Sensual They Kissed The Sun.
The summer stunned
With its uplifting rays of golden fire.
It warmed your spirit
And elevated it from dark corners
Within the icy corridors of winter
Where negative thoughts
Invaded your frozen conscious
The perfect breeding ground for misery.

We held hands, as we strolled the grey clouds away
"Let's leave the graveyard for the dead".
A long-forgotten smile resurfaced,
Released by summer's glow
It unveiled the old, serene you
Emaciated lips blossomed into fleshy folds
Soft and sensual,
They kissed the sun.

Janette Fenton

I Had A . . . Dream

I had a dream that Nigel Farage was king
He sat on a throne orb and sceptre in his hands
And at his feet lay the dead bodies of refugee children
I had a dream that Suella Braverman was Britannia
Trident in hand she stood at the edge of our shores
Repelling the war torn and needy as they sought shelter from our land
I had a dream that our government rounded up all of the people that they classed as undesirable
Put them on planes and sent them to camps in countries thousands of miles away
I had a dream that refugees were spat on in public, beaten, ridiculed and reviled by the general public for no other reason than they were foreign refugees
In my dream I wake up in a cell, condemned by my own conscience for cowardice and inhuman behaviour for not standing shoulder to shoulder with the people who are being so brutally treated by my own country
I am awake now it's my choice . . .

Mark Ingram

England's Gory

What would you do for the red white and blue?
Throw stones at a Muslim?
Spit on a Jew?
Raise hell with the many or care for the few?
What would you do for the Red, White and Blue?
What would you do for the Union Jack?
Sign a petition to send 'em all back?
The Serbs, and the Poles, and especially the blacks?
Oh, what would you do for the Union Jack?
And what would you do for the sweet English rose?
Is it ethnic cleansing that you propose?
This multiracial land is not what you chose?
Oh, what would you do for the sweet English Rose?
So what will you do for this country so fair?
Stand and be counted or don't you really care?
Till there's murder and chaos and civil war in the air?
Now what will you do for this country so fair?

Mark Ingram

I Chose To Wear Twigs

Not so skinny when under investigation, when albino
Bailiffs instigate liquidation, when straw from a barn
Ambitious new fashions
When abstaining from laughing morphs into opera
You see comedy in donning Ramones style, keep in the
Groove with showbiz types, trying not to advise the golden
Hour public, you lack conviction of your unexplained death
Take a guided tour, a silent disco
Gothic walking boogie tour
To see bullet holes and famous watering holes, and glory holes
And goofy grins, vainglorious, in chorus
The architect of your own affluent demise
Best for cognitive stuttering, prison cell window mutterings
Congregational mentality is the oyster burger buzz, lobster
Garnished with mayo and garlic, sipping
Glaswegian Gin, all
Bodes well for distillery experiences
Flanged with hapless tourists, aubergine tartlets, and railing
Against where it's at, those
Tartan outlets
You've met your match you pyromaniac, overlapping
Dracula
Tapping into the global recession, no mention of inconceivable
Hybrids, the horror of clones hypothetically living side-by-side
With original artists, evil God-like twists pulling wings off flies
Fruit flies, too
Not just any ugly glib bugger, superglued to tarmac, a genetic
Caricature, the first
Laurette dodging thoughts

Writing about bias, all kinds of unpublished gangs
Going on tour soon, without a safety net, without the elderly
Ho-hum it's cobweb time, minus repertoire, single-handedly
Kites adorn your darkening sky
And dismantle affected classrooms
Your dirty laundry and now a six part documentary,
In extremis
You don't have to be an actor to deliver a kiss like you mean it.

Meek

At That Moment

So happily drunk, here, dozens try to reinvent me
Sexual soreness is the sorriest to translate
Yielding to vulnerability, shying away from an inferiority
Complex, this weakness has no purpose
Being around you holds some potential, I think
I'm strong enough to resist all advances
For my room is lit, my wrists are cut, and my soul is hurt

It's not the wisdom in saying goodbye, it's not the
Unexpected nature of an unblessed escape
So gentle the inhalation, so tragic the desperation
I almost faint through detoxifying just as I'm about
To make myself clear
If you called today I'd heed your words, I'd stash the razors
In the bottom drawer

Later I discover the influence of your poor health, about
The remaining few friends seeking to be published
Your home is an abattoir, a twitching, living museum
Immune to the elapsing minutes, spread in your amusing limbs
Your physical spirituality is refuge for your enemies
I am jealous to these times and space, it takes love
To provide provisions

Desiring the nothingness I've ascribed to, that I've the strength
Gleaned from it
I cling to dreams and the unfounded accusations, find little
Solace after another glass or two
There's so much clearly that's been waylaid

I think, yes, I know you as being alive
I was warned about these decisions

Something like the possibility of recognition and wanting
To feed it, wanting to bleed your sleeping carcass dry
My fingers to the earth, to the dirt you breathe
I linger with the pack, pose with many whimsical mourners
On the face of it I have learned nothing, but felt the nails
Hammered into my flesh, you see, there's no one with intellect
Ready to listen

Not realising my current independence, I look to break each
Thought with fading grasps
I want answers, I want to be heard
Not smug last letters and death's beautiful words
For once I had dusk and memories of dust, once I tried
Psychoanalysis, and hung around longer, inarticulate
And at snail's pace

Whether to stick or whether to wander, whether to confront
Myself and create dissatisfaction
This attraction troubles me; it lets the crows, the hard bitten
Crows, espying a glimpse like would-be intruders
No one else even noticed the sky, or the lack of clouds,
Or the motionless crowd. No one stepped forward to stand alone,
or tried to continue.

Meek.

Penned This Morning

Guess I haven't learned
Any lessons from back then
Can't believe I'm falling
For the same old tricks again

Maybe I'm just stupid
This is such a big deal
'Cos I can't tell a lie
about the way you make me feel

My heart is on my sleeve
That's where it lives
Vulnerable and sensitive
It's a heart which truly gives

I should hide it away
Until the coast is clear
But it knows what it wants
And can sense when you are near

So here I go I know the drill
Just need to press repeat
I'll collect the broken pieces
As you drop them at my feet.

Susan Broadfoot

I Guess

I guess I could change
Rearrange turn a page
Drag it out
Scream and shout

So many times we tried
Cried and cried no alibi
Maybe friends
Go around again

It's really up to you
Change the things I do
I would do it for you
If you want me to

This time trying harder
Satisfying this hunger
Or Just let it be
Set us both free.

Ian OPG London

If Your High Takes Control

If your high takes control
It's time to just let it go
Maybe you won't ever know
When your gone no place left to go

Feels good out of your head
Feeling nothing when you're dead
When your high takes control
It's time to just let it go

We all like to escape
Drift away to another place
But when your high takes control
It's time to just let it go

Feel the warmth surround you
Relax and float drift away
But when your high controls you
It's time to just let it go

How many do you know?
We all like a little blow
But when that high takes control
It's time to just let it go.

Ian OPG London

rush hour @ the hospital

whos doing the drugs
whos doing the porridge
whos got the bedsheets together
whos filling in forms instead of caring
whos daughter is ill
whos boy or girl wants some appreciation
whos pay packet dont stretch two weeks
whos car is hungry
whos love life is falling apart
whos doing the drugs
whos doing the Weetabix
whos paying the parking fees
whos chasing their tail
whos being robbed
who wants to put their feet up
blindfold poems today .x

Denny Paul Mills

Dame Villanelle

My masquerade shows what I try to hide
in every winter garden's box-trimmed form.
They always go, Hiss! Boo! though I have tried.

No matter where I go, I am espied
before I duck or fade into a corm.
My masquerade shows what I try to hide.

If I disguise in blooms, they spread so wide
that all know - by my shape - I can't conform.
They always go, Hiss! Boo! though I have tried.

Sweet imperfections I cannot abide.
When I break free and dance, I must reform;
my masquerade shows what I try to hide.

They think I'm dated, but I've never lied
to be a buxom dame and flirt at norm.
They always go, Hiss! Boo! though I have tried.

This dame is not a villain, so I'll ride
the front end; Norman's ass will kick a storm.
My masquerade shows what I try to hide,
they always go, Hiss! Boo! though I have tried.

Wendy Webb

Disabled Toilet
Dawntreader/Issue 8/2009-09/PUBLD

Oh, the toilet seat, the toilet seat,
I'm surfing on the sea.
Oh, the toilet seat, the toilet seat,
it makes me feel so free.

Oh, the toilet seat, the toilet seat,
I carefully dare to sit,
then find myself wedged between love handles
that don't help a bit.

Oh, the toilet seat, the toilet seat,
when I want to take a leak,
the forward motion, side to side
all makes me feel quite weak.

Oh, the toilet seat, the toilet seat,
now I don't dare to push
and even worse, when I arise,
the toilet will not flush.

Wendy Webb

I Should 'Ave Looked After Me Teeth
2020-07/PUBLD Star Tips 138

So disappointed that she's on her own,
but looking forward to the show and pleased
that she is going anyway; instead of staying home.
To live a little, die a little, in her clouding thoughts.

She finds a parking space, reads the machine
and all around her, puzzled people queueing
in higgledy piggledy confusion of the sign
and what they had to pay and for how long.
She studied lengthy instructions, thought she understood
the price to pay and fumbled in her purse.

She did not want to keep them waiting long
and no-one else seemed sure what they should pay.
So rather than delay them further, coined
the slot machine with fumbling imprecision,
posting the full amount, for required hours;
allowing for the show to overrun.

The ticket vomited into her hand
as she stood staring at the exit time.
The machine had finally imprinted loud and clear
that she must leave in the interval,
before the show had run its course, to queue
and leave that packed theatre, reach her car,
or wonder whether she'd return to find
it clamped and immovable as that sign.

Returning to her car, she cried a little
and then a helpful woman walked across
and pointed out her error; quite precise
and how the puzzled queue now understood,
so wouldn't make the same mistake she'd made.

She fumbled with her mobile, phoned back home,
to rage severe distress with foghorn words
that made less sense to passers-by, though she
bled through her shame as they skipped, giggling past.

She listened to soft words, her husband's calm,
then shaking, reversed out of the parking space
with sobbing breaths, to focus on each gear
and happy audience crowds, now entering.
She calmed dull road rage into traffic lights
and circumnavigated roundabouts,
until her love sparked braver face
and then she parked and paid the fee again.

A miniscule amount, no raging crowds,
to park for hours past midnight - far too long -
and then she sat alone and looked around
at happy chatting faces, past that age
when all the world's a stage for youthful fun.
The men were mostly white; or slow; or hot;
and all those women's hairstyles were the same:
a mirror image of that comedienne,
all presence, trim, but - goodness - where were her teeth!

Wendy Webb

And I Must Go
2017-05/PUBLD Star Tips 119

The time is short and I must go,
the collared doves are calling
and butterflies are flitter-fluttering,
dancing in the light.

For time is short and I must go,
the sun is burning in the sky:
I wish I could stay.

The collared doves are crooning in the branches.
It's time to go, the sky is deepest blue
and wind is twitching restlessly, please stay!
I shiver, it is time.

The time of evening scent is rising now.
The dog barks, and the cat has found a corner
and no-one else thinks it is time to stay
in the garden.

Dream on, there's not a single cloud, nor haze,
tomorrow it could rain, it could be grey
and every moment could be full, as people are;
busy, too busy, to see.

Wendy Webb

Passing Time On A Spring Day
2017-03/PUBLD Star Tips 118

It is that time of the evening
when the curtains are closed,
and the second glass of red is emptying fast.
When everything is muggy, warm,
and life could not be better for a while.

It is the time to drink it to the dregs,
to watch Midsummer fade, so out of time,
and wonder when those April Showers will fall,
but not tonight, a bride's bouquet is thrown
to steamy sunsets rocking into dark.

It is the time for bridges, lost and found,
the time to wear the past, like Emperor's clothes
and laugh a little, cry a little, giggle

at long johns, hot pants, skimpy, light or Scottish,
and so to breeze to rest, beyond all dreams.

Wendy Webb

The Hours Are Passing Fast

2011/10/PUBLD, Partners/Oct 11; Partners Comp/Honours List/Oct 11

The sun sets now, so vividly with hope
as all the world sleeps on in endless summer
of wakefulness within the brain, to murmur
that it is time to rise. The world has spoken -

And we cannot imagine what will be.
What's left to dream? Should dreamers, waking, sleep?
There's much to do; less time to think, to keep
those memories alive. We cannot see

what has been lost; our powers, each step, each moment,
for sunlight sets while dreamers move each day:
like standing stones, they stretch and warp away.
That silence now is closing fast, and opened

as if the supermoon would never die.
And yet, the sleepers know - in dreams - it lies . . .

Wendy Webb

Extracting The Truth
PUBLD/2020-03 Crystal (116)

I'm visiting the dentist,
I've never been so scared.
I was here three weeks ago,
I don't know how I've dared.

Toothache is the fiercest thing,
thought it gingivitis,
now he says it was much worse
more painful than arthritis.

Hoped that I was being brave,
waited the appointment.
It was too much, too long, pain-free
was not a disappointment.

The locum checked the tooth I said,
pain spread in all directions.
But dentists like to know which one
before they start extractions.

A sad old tale, full three weeks long
is far too much to bear.
The tortured dentist needs to know:
tap-no, tap-ouch, tap-there.

The X-Ray neatly ticked his box:
it's far too near the nerve.

It's deep and not much tooth is left
to keep its life and verve.

It is the molar up there, not
the wisdom tooth you're taking?
I'm the expert, so don't tell me
which molar you're mistaking.

I'll loosen it. You can't feel that?
Oh no, I wouldn't dare.
And then it slid out like a slug
I didn't feel, anywhere.

I'm so relieved, still shaking,
I nearly wet the floor
and though his 'Well done' should be mine,
I'm just stumbling through the door.

I did not say the hearing aid
works best with clear instruction,
in front, not dentally above/behind
with panic-blanched compunction.

I took the cotton-pack to wadge,
in case it started bleeding.
In a country lay-by . . . Well,
. . . Officer, I was speeding

because a glob of mouth or gum
was spreading round my dentures –

though I don't have them yet, bright red
was spreading round my pearlies.

Don't make me breathe in that, this clot
is not for the fainthearted.
I need to bite down hard and wait
for the recently-departed . . .

second molar. Which one? It's gone,
now I'm bleeding like a vampire.
If you don't get this siren home,
she'll bloom like sweetest samphire. (pron: sam-fur)

Don't eat, but keep it sterile,
stay upright, and don't drink.
I'm feeling like an invalid
dripping black hole in the sink.

I have revived with liquid mush
on one side; the other dribbling.
There's only one thing scares me now -
the next dentist expert quibbling.

Wendy Webb

Earning A Gold Star Along The Road
Web Star/2021-12/WEB

Adrenaline pulsing through arteries of tarmac,
there – on an impulse – darting to the flow:
two trailer-slatted loads, pulled tractor-slack.
I saw the learner driver going slow.

There on an impulse, darting to the flow,
with oncoming traffic flashing, hurtling fast,
I saw the learner driver going slow;
braced for bomb-blast debris flying past.

With oncoming traffic flashing, hurtling fast,
the L-Plate slid between each tractioned load.
Braced for bomb-blast debris flying past;
held back by jellied legs that might explode.

The L-Plate slid between each tractioned load;
I contemplated dreams from late last night:
held back by jellied legs that might explode,
guessed he saw me moving into sight.

I contemplated dreams from late last night,
so hugged him close and much too long to grieve.
Guessed he saw me moving into sight;
happy to be there. Now he had to leave,

so I hugged him close and much too long to grieve;
found a golden star on bathroom floor.

Happy to be there, now he had to leave.
Sun sparkled morning light through that brash door.

Found a golden star on bathroom floor,
two trailer-slatted loads pulled tractors slack.
Sun-sparkled morning light through that brash door;
adrenaline pulsing through arteries of tarmac.

Wendy Webb

Whitby (Villanelle)
2020-10/PUBLD Star Tips Xtra

Where memorabilia magic sets the tone,
radio songs bring sadness on the wing;
The Abbey Steps Tea Room leaves my breaths alone.

With cosy seats and warmth till gasping's done,
black cats and broomsticks can't make all hearts sing,
where memorabilia magic sets the tone.

Yet tea and coffee's comforting as home;
cakes don't cost the earth: your children bring,
The Abbey Steps Tea Room leaves your breaths alone.

There's lollipops and snacks, so climbers come,
those 199 steps hold much less sting,
where memorabilia magic sets the tone.

All tourists at the bottom – each a stone –
attempts this captured window-gazing's spring.
The Abbey Steps Tea Room leaves their breaths alone.

Exhausted beneath St Mary's, where you lie prone,
consider tea and cake (reign as a king,
where memorabilia magic sets the tone.
The Abbey Steps Tea Room leaves my breaths alone.

Wendy Webb

Spring Forward (Villanelle, 2021-2024)
Web Star/2022-03

Easter '24 wears vivid sunshine,
the calm before an Arctic blast, foretold.
Sweet daffodils – all shades – dressed tulips define

pouting lips and stars' fire, that refine
the wild and Northern wind which hails fresh cold.
Easter '24 wears vivid sunshine,

we garden with heaven's vengeance as sublime,
so pray that dancing drifts reclaim their gold.
Sweet daffodils (all shades). Dressed tulips define

that mercilessness storms revoke, resign.
Now, shrubs and flowers, stand proud and be bold,
Easter '24 wears vivid sunshine.

May summer's heat return their shades of time,
so fickle gardeners rest; their toils behold.
Sweet daffodils – all shades – dressed tulips define.

Redeem the year that's gone as days combine
the warmth that's in our hearts, and now enfold.
Here star '24 wears vivid sunshine,
sweet petunias – all shades – dressed dahlias define.

Wendy Webb

Selections Of Limericks

Ancient Town of Snotting
Have you heard of the great town of Snotting,
full of lace, men in tights and trainspotting.
Thank the gods for invasion,
dialect Hams through the nation.
Drop the 'S', take up Footie/goal-popping.

50 Shades of High Noon
They say, write what you know: 50 shades,
so I started with dawn's latest raids.
The staff were gem-happy,
tried 60, changed nappy.
Hid 20, for aroma pervades.

Aerial Installations
There's a man with a van makes connections,
he'll deliver, install, give directions.
So please flag him down now,
he promises, and how,
his strap line says: 'Guaranteed erections.'

Wendy Webb

Holidays Are Hellish

Oh, do not go on holiday,
everything is back at home.
The brochure has a tempting way
of encouraging you to roam.
No sooner has a day; a night
Passed. . . and hellish confirmed your fears,
than counting days until your flight
back home's the only thing that cheers.

The kitchen is spectacular,
chairs scream off a perfect tiled floor.
The bedroom's calm vernacular
springs a dawn chorus through the door.
The view's to die for - nearly mort -
Wainwright panoramas coerced.
Fine dining . . . can the rich be bought?
The Chippy queue has been rehearsed.

The WiFi code/or key safe lags,
garden's mortgaged to the neighbours.
There's Artisan pricing shop tags.
Boot - twice-packed - defies all labours.
The cost of your reluctant wee
post-tea/coffee/juice or cider,
card only payments: 50p,
soap spurts to floodtide of water.

Wendy Webb

Fortitude

Sometimes it's enough to be here
Sometimes it's OK to be not OK
Sometimes it's time to let go
Sometimes carrying on is a trial
Sometimes carrying on seems impossible
Sometimes carrying on takes everything you have
Sometimes carrying on seems pointless
But carrying on proves that you are a marvel
A triumph of spirit over seemingly terrible obstacles
A victory over adversity
Sometimes carrying on is all you can do
But by carrying on we inspire
We galvanise
We defy the odds
We show the way to others who also feel helpless
So carry on and carry on some more
Because you are a winner
And the prize will be yours
If you keep carrying on.

Mark Ingram

Cirrhosis Of The Heart

Don't know where the end is
Don't know where to start
I've a fractured sense of justice
And cirrhosis of the heart
Can't see straight for looking
My brain is blown apart
Morally I'm bankrupt.
I've cirrhosis of the heart
My nerves are beyond shattered
Blood pressures off the chart
A temper like a typhoon
And cirrhosis of the heart
Doctor says its terminal
I say he's a tart
I can live for years and years and years
With cirrhosis of the heart.

Mark Ingram

Tension

Tension such tension
Keep job?
Early pension?
Sickness!!!
Uncertainty!!!
What will change?
Is it cancer?
Is it real?
Am I a chancer?
What if inconclusive?
Then what?
A fraud-No
Its real, I feel it
I'm scared
Because I'm not frighten
Tension, and this is the tip
But what of;
The tip of the iceberg that sinks my Titanic?

Mark Ingram

On The Level

Neither up nor down
Extremis no likely
I would like to be level
Neither tyrant nor clown
Plateau unlikely
Not angel or devil
It's a lifelong ambition
Being boring appeals
A face in the crowd desired
A break with tradition
Just to know how it feels
I'd like a complete rewire
So what does it take?
How to proceed?
Is there a simple solution?
Or I am cursed to remain?
Forever the same?
A one man internal contusion.

Mark Ingram

After A Good Day For Ice Cream

After a good day for ice cream at the police station.

Upon the very likely event of me ever being dead.

I have drawn up a schedule of service or special events or a list of dos and don'ts.

If I must have a box and I expect that I will for no other better reason than modesty.

Make it a cheap one cardboard will do or at a push recycled cut up cereal boxes.

I want to be cremated if it isn't too expensive, if it is find a man who keeps pigs or use the fire pit I bought years ago.

As far as I know we've only used once and it seems such a shame not to get some use.

You can do me on the grill a bit at a time. Throw any left-over ash on the garden or better still on the veg.

Don't have a service no eulogies please I'm trying to enjoy being dead.

I don't need you all reminding yourselves of all the dumb things that I have said.

Don't have a party, or better still if you must make sure everyone gets minging drunk and end up fighting in the garden. Preferably on the veg.

Kicking up the newly scattered ash into the alcoholic fug.

To be carried away on the pork chop smelling breeze that used to be me.

It will be back in the morning, and so night time is a good enough reason

To be honest with you.

Sweet dreams and sleep.

Upon the likely event I get home safe.

I'll take it easy

A simple day ahead -

1. See what you can see for yourself, not so much daydreaming. Be sure to have a new phone so you can see the future, a good brand name for once.

2. Later today, be honest with myself.

3. Things I came to terms with.
I will never see Iggy live and The Son of Man I don't want you to be there.

4. In a while now you will know what it all means, I never excluded being wrong.
I had the chance of this and that and I will be 'late' now.

5. Watch out! If I have to get old, tonight and tomorrow then I have a couple days to kill.

For my boys:

6.May the people of this country stop viciously turning on their glorious years of play in English gardens just to take a job that pays enough for the sake of appearances.

7. I will not walk in and crawl out of my life and away from the deaths of my friends. Whilst dignified types divest them of dignity and the superannuated sweat of their brow. Are they the same people who coined the phrase; go to work on an egg?
Make them send the nest-egg they owe you in time to pay for your shroud?

8. I had a new life in the end; I had to admit that you and I turned out the same.

9. Doctor, will you get back to me with your new number the day before my next appointment with you? I might not be able to come in to therapy.

10. For the sake of my favourite living authors: Say a bit more about the alternative side-effects of divine mercy on me.

That's how the Armageddon hustle is made fit for purpose.
You have a one person who can do the needful task, for the sake of the many.
Push the cloud up and out, wait long enough and the cloud will fall
But my clouds are always rising on the other side of the hill.

Another 10. I will change my mind and heart and I will be cleaner before you finish this line.
And even if it is, only for the sake of vanity let the fallen lie.

Des Lane

The Make Do Man

She has a library of photo albums
Full of legends from before his time
Did he even exist until he met her?
Scanned, stamped, catalogued, dated,
Reviewed by her peers and family, laminated?
Moving in the perpetual now, he can never be a longing.
He is her make do man.
Along with scenes playing out her past,
Locations and people, before he was cast Charisma and wit calligraphically penned for everyone to see.
Their voices timbre, lilt or burr brightly described in Chroma key
But whilst looking for his own intellect's portrayal he found it wasn't part of his role, his place in the troupe was decoratively physical.

His future is knowing he will never be a longing
When a conversation set her heartbeat racing he wasn't even present.
He has been unskilled by the passions of her past
He is a make do man

Every day is a page in his new book.
Some pages he goes back to, re-reads and smiles.
Some entries he tears out and burns
But some that he turns to, make him think
He should have left them blank.
He will never be a longing, he'll never be a could-have been so good.

She'll take a call and for an hour she's in her element.
Although her voice is hushed when she responds
While she's on the phone her happiness is obvious.
She'll never laugh like that for him
He doesn't share their book of recollections.
All he can hope for are passing nods and the chorus of 'that's nice'

He doesn't keep a diary now he's cut it down to making lists of all the things he knows he is.
The Fill in
The mark time
The substitute
The hard rebound
The never to be her lost longing.
The wish it could have been.
He is her make do man.

Des Lane

The Poet and The Circus Strongman

Sometimes words are weights dragging me down into the harsh belly of creativity. Liquefying weights solidifying inside my desk, heavy with cries of. . . "Not today. Please not, not, not, today!"

Corrugated iron ideas crusting around the iris of each blood shot eye, I spy with my little eye crushing creativity of an ink stained diminishing cusp.

I lift these weights. Inhale, exhale, and grunt spasmodic, incoherent words of encouragement defying its rage I stab my pen into the centre of the page break through bone and cartilage, pierce the heart and, and, and breathe I catch a quick reflection of circus strongman in the glass on my desk.

John Mcmahon

This Is The Land

From womb we came to enter a room of white. Faces, a world of faces. Their eyes tell the truth, no matter how big their smiles are. . .

This is the land of shifting sand. Bad weather. Sure it's all smiles now; it will be for a while. But soon the sand will shift to sinking sand - you will be buried waist deep in tiny grains of pain... Unless you're protected, but few are in the end you'll face the reality of this world and its Bi-polar personality.

This is the land you have been made to be part of: Hunger, famine, disease flying through the air a million flapping bumble bees

Stinging
Stinging
Stung!

Remember

We came together to remember
to dance, to hold hands
to hold the room with a single

Breathe.

John Mcmahon

Walk By The River

Break of day the same again
Sunlight streaks the windowpane
Streets that shine from falling rain
Still no change
The chase in vain
Again.
Walk by the river watching the flow
No work today.

Empty days as a lifetime flies
Another meal and a mother sighs
Children ask why father cries
They don't know
How low you go
So low.

Working out just what you need
Clothes to wear and mouths to feed
Let's forget the Christmas tree
We'll get by
I know we've tried
And tried.

Blame the economy
For stolen dignity
Take me away
Watch the river flow.

Janette Fenton

Anonymous

There you lie
Day after day
Night after night
Anonymous.
In a donated duvet
Wet through and
Tucked in tight-
So tight
I almost stepped on you.
Tight, into the stone cold wall
You shelter
Between the railway arch and the street
To escape the winds that oppress you.
The tunnel visioned passers by
Pass by you
As they pass you by
Unfazed.
You have become a feature of the landscape
Anonymous.
No longer novel enough
To cause a reaction.
Stonewalled
In this wind tunnel of our society
You cry for help
To relieve the biting wind
That takes chunks out of your soul
Like some Bully dog mauling at your flesh.

Anonymously
I gave you something

To ease your discomfort;
A token gesture,
A woolly hat,
A wrap- around scarf,
Some loose change.
Bully for me!

I felt better though
As I snuggled into my warm, dry duvet
In my warm, dry bed
In my warm, dry bedroom
Where the cold stone wall
Keeps the cold out.

Janette Fenton

Our Rainbow Shone In Autumn Winds

Autumn winds
blew through our wastelands
of self-defeat
and hurled us together
in our need of need.
In silent embraces
our lost souls
clung to dark edges.
We took refuge there.
Swept into each other's arms
we slept walked
into a black hole
that trapped our light
and captured our tears.
United in internal reflection
Our rainbow shone.

Janette Fenton

Wound Up

I am tired and I would sleep
but I can cannot shut my eyes
I hesitate at edge of night
for when I put the day away
tomorrow's emptiness is near

In afternoon I craved to lie
within the comfort zone of bed
The world awake closing in
Indians circling the single cart

But now that all have gone to sleep
deep arrows keep the mind from rest
although that mind wants thought to cease

Clinging to the edge of night
I am tired but cannot sleep.

George Colkitto

On Swithering Heights (choosing between Roast Beef and Tongue at Morrisons)

I have attained Swithering Heights
or have I?
Perhaps I am on the plains of uncertainty
yet to climb the foothills of indecision?
I have journeyed so long, or does it just feel
that time is endless? Has it been short?
Maybe somewhere in between, neither
one nor the other?
Recalling the ups and downs, more up than down,
alternatively more down than up.
This could be the valley of procrastination and not
the high ground I thought.
Emily where are you? Come make certain
that I am indeed on the moors of lost paths
hesitating on the edge of Swithering Heights.

George Colkitto

Till The Curtain Drops

What do you do when it's all gone wrong
when the dancers twirl and they sing your song
but you cannot move and the legs won't work.
You sit and swear and curse your luck.

The beat is rousing, you want to sing
but the voice which rises has a hollow ring.
Out of tune and strangled cat
who in the world would smile at that.

You look around for the mate to hug
You're on your own by the fireside rug
and the fire is out and the room is cold
And so are you. You once so bold

Now shiver naked by the ashes blowing
exposed and bare, your inadequacies showing.
Once another would call your name.
Once another would hide your shame.
But now alone, empty and drawn
is there a reason for life to go on?

What do you do when the music stops
but wait for the moment when the curtain drops.

George Colkitto

In Sand

Draw lines
childhood fantasies
spade marks on the sand
shapes and words
cricket pitches
excited swirls
love hearts
take twigs
sculpt a face
scratch out eyes
and with the passing years
the ebbs and flows
tears will smudge the edges
tides carry them away.

George Colkitto

Parallel Universe

Like Schrödinger's cat
the box is shut, no-one can see
inside
You are alive and you are dead

Outside is isolated
there is a lid to neither world
proof that nothing matters
for it reconvenes, multiplies

I should cheer for you are
in a parallel universe
divided from the other
in which I choose to cry.

George Colkitto

Jimmy, Can Ye Spare Me A Rhyme
(*Breathes there the man with soul so dead*)

I could hae been a poet, but I dinnae know it
I thought I dinnae hae the wurds
Nane o yon fancy vocabulary

I'd hae joined the constabulary
but in ma day, I wus tae wee.
Just a dunt o'er five fit
an six fit was whit thae wantit.
Thae platform heels hadnae been inventit.
a Bobby in stilettos. Nae way!

Sae I had tae find something else tae dae
The burru is fine fae a while but ye canna smile
wi empty pockets. Nae brass means nae lass.
Worse still nae booze and youse know
a Scotsman wi na swally is a poor pal, eh
in the dreich close of life

I goat a job an' a wife
Ye know it wisnae aw it was cracked up to be
Aw thae tails when ye were a boy aboot bein a man
The craik, the wemin, the booze, kinda evapourate and lose
appeal in the steamie o life. I could make a killin'
if I had a shillin for every disappointment

Pain, ye dinnae know the haulf. There ain't nae ointment
can ease the piles ave sat on, stood in, shiftit.
I cannae claim ony ships, or engineering marvel craftit

by my haund, but ave wept oceans in bitter winds
that have frozen the lugs aff hope and blown up and doon
the Khyber Pass o' this Jock Tamson's bairn.

Sae dinnae walk on by wi a shrug nae carrin'
I could be you, ye numptie. Am nae the only Humpty Dumpty
in Scotland. Ah'm pairt o an army o' nutters and chancers
waitin for something, anything, a wee haun up

Ye know maybe I could still be a poet after aw.
a symbol of national recovery. Like yon upturned pile
o boats in Edinburgh. A new start on the seas
a voyage into tomorrow. A Pam Ayers oh the heather,
Hawd on and gies us a wurd oh encouragement
Say Jimmy, Can ye spare a rhyme.

George Colkitto

Flowers For The Girl

Why not give your crush a red, red rose
Share some feelings and see how it goes
Make your words complimentary and feminine
Make them serenade like the scent of Jasmine
Raise her heart up to the status of goddess
Give her an exotic orchid to match her finesse
But alas there is no beauty to compare to thee
No flowers or words in the dictionary that I can see
Lovely, delicious, delectable, desirable or divine
Intelligent, smart, canny, brilliant, intuitive or fine
Your heart knows what flowers to bring in this dream
Wild bluebells and snowdrops for your queen
A walk in the wilderness amongst the golden rays
May your love last forever until the end of days

Steven Joseph McCrystal

Moonbeams And Daydreams

Do all dreams shine like moonbeams?
A little touch a lunacy from the night
A wish made from within your dreams
A wish made when travelling into the light
Sunshine or rainbows or wishing upon a star
Have no permanence but lunacy will take you far
Night after night and day after day
The moon will shine in its indelible way
Possessing your mind with promises from the deep
Enticing actions only your intoxicated body can keep
Possessed by a dream in the waking hours
Lunacy might become your lover and bring you flowers
The more you dance in amongst the moonbeam bowers
The more you dance in amongst the storms and showers.

Steven Joseph McCrystal

The Chase Hurdles

Before you get to the reality of rejection
Be aware, there are hurdles in front of your flirtations
Don't be too needy a desperate man dies
Don't be too sensitive a delicate man cries
Don't be too pushy an insistent man starts fires
Don't be too flirty a salacious man fails
Don't be too slow but be patient so love can grow
Don't be too cool she could turn to ice
Don't listen to the advice of your friends
They'll get it wrong again and again
Don't listen to my advice because I'm stuck in limbo
Don't listen to my advice because I'm stuck in limbo
Scared to move in case I blow it. Simple
Once, twice, and thrice around the lover's bend
All arms and legs and head akimbo
Something I'm prone to in the end
Listening to all the does and don'ts my friend
Of my rejection demons guarding my feelings
My heart pumping you just need to be honest
Check the hurdles again you're running through a forest
Keep it simple, be yourself, and once again be honest
That's the best advice I can give but if opportunity knocks
Take your time, you'll grow on her, something you always do
So don't be a klutz and just pull up your socks
And straighten all those hurdles you've already ran through.

Steven Joseph McCrystal

Dragonflies

Ghostly, omni-directional,
Stirring micro-paths
Twisting through Summer's
Fragrant Jungles of blossom:

Alighting weightless,
Spider-limbs quiver
Beneath a fragile form,

Reflecting morning glimmers
On hazy ponds
Of rippled light;

Delicate as sunshine:
Folding gossamer wings
Under drooping fronds of willow.

Young girl reclines
In dappled shadow,
Hears a soft fluting
Of wind-song, drifting

Through tall reeds,
Directed
At the delicate insect -

Flitting darkly past her slender legs,
Like some fairy of herself;
Illuminated briefly

By Heaven's
Golden fire.
Two Dragonflies
In a birdsong morning.

David Norris-Kay

(Included in his collection,
'From Time-Buried Years)

Exit

(Royal Hospital, Sheffield, 1970)

The door to freedom is locked
with the key of pain.
Tissue-gnawing fear and uncertainty,
like diver's ballast,
weigh the body down
on a strange bed.
The human tide
has washed him broken on a shore
devoid of personality.
Only diseases exist here,
neatly categorised and guarded
by strict doctrine.
His visitor's offerings
of pantomime-smiles, are gestures
false as the doctor's
whispered euphemisms.

Birds still sing in his dreams,
where he walks whole and healthy,
proud as Casanova,
bearing his trophies
of chastened girls:
A stirring of libido
is extinguished by the smell of death,
in air that once rang
with the throaty birth-cries
of his entrance.
The featureless ceiling

which he knows better
than his own wrinkled hands,
reflects the pale light
of a vanishing sun.

David Norris-Kay

Ecology

I once saw a young girl with innocent ways,
Skipping through the sunset of childhood's long days,
Her manner was carefree, she stood on a rise,
Watching tall chimneys paint watercolour skies.

The thick smoke rose higher in dark mushroom clouds
And song birds were dying in smog-laden shrouds:
Still stood the young girl where the river flowed free,
Sliding over land to an oil-blackened sea..

The world builds for greed and the need becomes strong,
To sacrifice right in the favour of wrong,
And someone among us will fight till he's won
Control of the atoms which govern the sun.

The young girl is growing, a woman she'll be,
Exposed as her countrymen lose heart and flee,
From graves they are digging and hope that has gone,
To threats of destruction they've christened 'The Bomb'.

Now children are playing in innocent jest,
Their sounds drift to me as I gaze to the west,
Where night slowly darkens and no one asks why
Smoke is still drifting through the star-powdered sky.

David Norris-Kay

(I originally wrote this as song lyrics for my wife to write music to and sing on the folk clubs in the 1970s)

Sun Song

See the Spring from far away,
Bringing sun to your shaded face,
That's seen the lights shine through Winter,
In every near and distant place.

Storms have washed the seasoned parks,
Where Summer finds its chosen land
And as I walk the weathered paths
I feel my loved ones tender hand.

Shadows spreading where I tread,
Like laughter on a battlefield -
My open eyes are filled with light,
The power of which I hope to wield.

Sunlight take me to your havens,
Spread your ripples through my mind,
Poorer men have shed their rags,
Left their begging bowls behind.

Woods I love the way you waver,
Like a sylvan song in Spring,
Like a child in youth's disguises,
Time will take the hope you bring.

David Norris-Kay

[Inspired by walking through
Richmond Park. Sheffield,
with my wife, Adéle]

Autumn Clouds

Autumn clouds slide in unnoticed
and then suddenly the sun is gone.
You celebrate your birthday at this time
I wonder who will raise his glass to you
and look deep into those eyes
hoping for a glimpse of your elusive soul.
I remember we took shelter from a
sudden hail storm in Florence once
and we drank Guinness by the Arno
on one of your birthdays long ago.
Soon the days will shorten
and autumn will turn to winter.
I wonder where you will go
when the rains come this year.

Jon Bickley

Self

Some people think things are the thing
that their aspiration will be met
by the accumulation of objects.
A beautiful home, a car or two,
clothes that maketh the model life.

They imagine other people looking at
pictures of their home and being impressed.
So impressed that they are somehow
elevated by being in that home.

"Oh, look at them, they must be so happy."

Soon concrete will fall from the school ceiling
Low wages and an exhausted workforce
will make hospitals a dangerous place to go
and before you know it, public ownership cannot be trusted.

So you buy schooling, healthcare,
law and order. But you can't keep up.
You will never keep up.

They have you on a wheel.
Running and running.
Round and round.
Until you stop.
Dizzy.
Disillusioned.
Desperate to get off the wheel.
And when the disciple is ready

the salesman will appear
to sell you a self-help wheel.

Jon Bickley

Sixty

When we were young
life happened to us
pregnancy, parents divorced
mental illness
romantic breakups

By the time you are sixty
some of that has fallen away.
The party is being held
in someone else's house
and you chose not to go.

You can look back all you like
but sooner or later
you are going to have to
get used to the silence
and the fact that you are on your own.

An archway of fire
stands before you
beyond that
impenetrable darkness
you walk through that alone.

Jon Bickley

The Leaves Are Still Green

The leaves are still green
but the blossom has gone
there is white in my beard
and it will not be long
before the leaves cover my lawn
and somewhere under the same star
you settle a canvas on an easel,
are the leaves still green
where you are?

Jon Bickley

Waiting For Spring

Recovering from the operation
kept me indoors all Summer.
When the canopy was green
and dappled sunlight
was desiccated upon
the woodland floor.
When the hands of the leaves
flapped against each other
clapping the work of the sun
in its high office directly overhead.

I learned to swing on my two crutches
lightly on the right, firmly on the left
giving me partial use of my legs
but taking away the use of my hands.
How do I carry toast from the kitchen
to my desk
while clutching the crutches?
Rules, like hips, are there to be broken.

Soon leaves and crutches will fall away
and I will venture out into the October night.
I will learn to walk again in Winter,
while the trees are thinking about
what to do next.
I will try new dance steps
in the darkness.
I will watch how other people do it
and I will be the magpie
taking the steps that suite

the new me.
The new me in the old coat and hat
with a rooted step,
a budding pen,
waiting for Spring.

Jon Bickley

Goodbye, Jazzy Cat

The sun shone for you today
Your favourite thing on this Earth
You soaked up its rays
As always
It guided you with its healing glow
Towards the afterworld that awaits.

Josh was kind and thoughtful
As we watched the sun set in your eyes
Vibrant,
They did not dim
As they synchronised with the setting sun
We said our last goodbye.

Janette Fenton

Alan
1954 – 1970
(Killed In A Motorcycle Crash)

Youth is laughter:
And you laughed
as I lay with my love
among dim lights,
enmeshed in the sounds
of psychedelia.

You rode the saddle
of a freedom that scorned girls,
gauntlet-hands gripping steel,
trailing highways of laughter
through grey light:

Your bones lie severed
in an abstract of twisted chrome,
and still in quiet hours I hear
the laughter of your early death
mocking my rejection by love,
and the awful
rotting Winter of the years.

David Norris-Kay

Burbage

(Peak District Moors)

Cooled lava slabs table the brown,
where white cloud's fists clench in deep blue,
their conspiracies of breezes.

Mix these mists in the darknesses
which span me: Where thunderheads build
in high cradles of memory.

Where one slip could send me rolling
down stone-strewn slopes: Into futures
drowning in crippling pains of age.

Grey and black vapours consume me:
Fog the ambitions of my thought
down a hidden warren of years.

Crows like a shoal of shadowed fish:
Frightened: Flap in my weathered wake,
painting the bleak moonscape with life.

Now, brief hopes hover their bright ghosts
through this wild land's echoing caves,
blending Burbage with future dreams.

David Norris-Kay

The Monday Club

Into the past I meander,
Peter Callaghan and Andy Alexander.
Whichever pub with whichever brew,
Monday arrives and Mick does, too.
Beers in hand,
Govanhill, the promised land.
Queens Park/Celtic; Celtic/Queen's Park.
But holy shit! Don't go out after dark.
Nowadays. . .
Nowadays underground gangs,
With snarling fangs,
Drink in our stead.
Raise a glass to our one now dead.
And the south of my city,
Still vibrant and pretty;
A place to forget.
The happy memories,
A distant regret.

Michelle Carr

Silent Chaos

I have a secret
Yes, my secret
Never to betray
Haunting me constantly
As I'm thinking
Pray you can't hear
Reading my thoughts is my greatest fear

Whisper to my conscience, have a quiet word
Trying not to listen
Like I haven't heard

It could ruin all things
Hate to let you know
Shift the whole dynamic
Turn the volume way down low

There's a silent chaos in my mind
What am I to do? I'm in love with you
Searching for a peace I'll never find
What am I to do? I'm in love with you

Whisper to my conscience
Have a quiet word
Trying not to listen
Like I haven't heard

It could ruin all things
Hate to let you know

Change the whole dynamic
Turn the volume way down low

There's a silent chaos in my mind
What am I to do? I'm in love with you
Searching for a peace I'll never find
What am I to do?
I'm in love with you.

Susan Broadfoot

My Heart

Guess I haven't learned
Any lessons from back then
Can't believe I'm falling
For the same old tricks again

Maybe I'm just stupid
This is such a big deal
'Cos I can't tell a lie
about the way you make me feel

My heart is on my sleeve
That's where it lives
Vulnerable and sensitive
It's a heart which truly gives

I should hide it away
Until the coast is clear
But it knows what it wants
And can sense when you are near

So here I go I know the drill
Just need to press repeat
I'll collect the broken pieces
As you drop them at my feet.

Susan Broadfoot

Light

I see your light on
In the dead of night
Wondering what you're up to
My imagination takes flight

Torturing myself
who's receiving your attention?
Is it someone
I've ever heard you mention?

My light is also on
Perhaps you can see
My lips moving as I whisper
"*It used to be me*"

Susan
Susan Broadfoot

We keep our love in the darkness
As we don't want anyone to know
I wish, just once, I could see your face
Watch your feelings show

As to you I surrender
Let emotions run free
Silently acknowledge
This is how it has to be

We keep our love in the darkness
It just has to be this way

It would all be over
If exposed to the light of day.

Susan Broadfoot

Double Take

You watched me, your twin sister, brush my long, golden hair in the mirror, as you did every night before bedtime, mesmerised by the slow careful strokes of the brush caressing the thick mass of gold. We were identical in every way, same eyes, same cheeky smile, freckles.

"Lights out now," called mum from the hallway.

You shouted, "Good night," to mum and whispered "Goodnight," to me although we continued to whisper for a while.

We eventually dropped off to sleep.

The next morning, mum reminded you that you had to attend a hospital appointment in the afternoon so you would have to be out of school sharp. Oh yes. The hospital. How you despised that place but you had to go. You were ill and they would make you better. Deep down you knew this but you didn't like being in the building full of wards of ill patients. Even the rustle of the crisp clean uniforms of the nurses disturbed you. I suppose it served as a reminder that you were ill, very ill. You didn't want to be reminded of that.

Still, you had me, your twin for support. I would always cheer you up after hospital visits and we would giggle into the night about the cold hands of the doctor, or the scary nursing sisters, or the handsome porters.

Our parents had always been truthful about your illness. They answered your questions as openly and honestly as they could. The doctors were very good too. You were so young to be coping with such a terrible disease but so far, you seemed to be coping very well. So far.

You were a natural worrier. You worried when having to attend the hospital because sometimes it was during school hours and that meant you missed out on lessons. You worried that you would forget to take your medication at the right time. You worried that you might have to cope with dreadful pain. Worry, worry, worry.

I didn't seem to inherit this trait however. According to you, I remained calm, collected and in control at all times. You really admired this about me. I was so strong, you said.

We went everywhere together; inseparable, sharing our secret hopes and desires. You always wanted to be a ballet dancer. In fact, you were attending ballet classes until you began to tire easily, so the doctors advised that perhaps it was too much for you at the moment. This came as a great disappointment. However, you never gave up on your dreams, imagining yourself en pointe, in a beautiful tutu, floating across the stage in a famous production one day. You lived to dance.

You waited at the school gate for mum to collect you, but not for long. Mum was there in seconds. Another natural worrier. She didn't like to keep people waiting so the pair of you rushed off to the hospital.

"How have you been today love?" she asked in the car on the way.

"A bit tired today mum. Everything is such an effort but I'm fine." You replied as you squeezed mum's hand as you always did in your reassuring way.

After the appointment, you came to our room, to tell me about your day and to tell me about the new drugs you had been given by the doctor. You knew that whatever they had tried before had not worked so they were adopting a different approach. I told you not to worry and that the doctors were on your side, fighting your cause. You gave me a hug and you thanked me for the re-assurance. Again, there was the nightly ritual of hair brushing then going to bed.

A few months later, the illness had progressed to such an extent that you had to spend longer and longer in hospital. The nurses were amazed at the change in your attitude and that you had such a fighting spirit for someone as young. You always seemed so positive. They said you were a real tonic to have around, even though you really were not well. The other patients often commented on your sunny disposition. At night you would talk at length to me, discussing your ups and downs, hopes and fears. We would fall asleep in each other's arms.

One day, mum was called to the hospital to be told that there was nothing else that could be done and that it would not be long now. She hugged you very tightly and told you over and over again how much she loved you and that you were very brave. You hugged mum back as tightly as you could. You didn't have to say anything. You knew, you just knew.

Two weeks later, you watched me brush my hair for the last time. It was hard to say goodbye to you but you knew it wouldn't be forever. It would only be a temporary separation.

When you died it was peacefully in your sleep. The nurses asked mum if she would like to take away your things. They also asked why I had never been to visit you whilst in hospital, her sister. Mum said you didn't have a sister. The nurses had been convinced that you did. A twin. Identical. The realisation spread over mum's face as it dawned on her what they meant. You and I were born twins, but sadly I never made it past 24 hours. You survived. Mum never told you about me. She thought it best that you didn't know, but you always knew didn't you? I was your secret.

Hundreds of people attended your funeral today. Everyone loved you. I was so proud of you. Mum dressed you in a beautiful nightdress she had bought for you, which you had never worn, and your favourite ballet shoes. She also put two other things in beside you, your hairbrush and your wig. How you loved brushing that wig, in the mirror, talking to me, your twin sister. I was always with you, right to the end. Now it's a new beginning.

Goodnight. See you in the morning.

Susan Broadfoot

Fall Is Falling

When you sit outside in the autumn air...
"What's that? Can you spot it? It's over there!
"It's a hedgehog, don't you see?"
"It's over there rustling in the leaves!"
Outside the creaking trees are naked,
"Let us get some brownie mix and bake it."
Go to Tesco and grab your autumn home decor,
Come back home before you get more and more.
Sitting with your dog crossed legged by the fire,
The winds whistle in a choir.
As the long day comes to an end,
Get cosy in bed while the trees in the wind bend.
While the foxes are calling,
Fall is falling.

Robyn Isobel Florence McEwan

Red Jacket

Red jacket,
September, October, November, not December are the fall months of the year.
The crunch of the leaves spears your ears.

Red jacket,
"I know it's a cold feel but I can give you "warm tones"."
Suggests the Aldi home decor worker.

Red jacket,
The leaves waltz down the tree hitting every move,
They work together in a groove.

Red jacket endless and ire,
We crunch and crackle in unison as we resemble fire.

Robyn Isobel Florence McEwan

Looking Back At Me

Looking back at me

What do I see?

What has become of me?

What do you see?

What version of me

Shall I be?

A scene of apathy

Insincerity bullshit me

Surrounding me

Speak to me

Help me

Fuck me

Love me

Nothing me

What do I see

Looking back at me?

Ian OPG London

Betrayal

You didn't understand me.

We were worlds apart.

Yet in my youth we were close and together

I betrayed you.

You never forgave or forgot.

Your anger ran deep within.

In illness I was needed.

In death I was forgotten.

Patricia Bell

Gentle Man

I forgot you in the noise of everyone else.

You came through and gently showed your face.

Happy memories of childhood came flooding back.

Guilt overwhelmed me.

Forgetting you in all the chaos

Of those who needed to be heard.

Patricia Bell

Ode To Man

Earth is struggling.
But those in power don't care.
It is shaking in fear.
Burning in rage
Howling in pain
Drowning in tears
Who is listening to its cry.

The ants are helpless against the giants.
Anger and frustration is building
They try in their own way to be heard.
But the enormity is too great.

They say nature is resilient.
But even nature is helpless in their battle.
The Earth will shake, burn, howl and drown.
Until man and nature is no more
Then new life will begin.

Patricia Bell

Circus

The ring master with the broken whip
holds the crowd by their finger tips
he doesn't want them to know
that he will never let them go.

Giancarlo Moruzzi

Holy Flame

Are we lost
Inside a holy flame?
Can we reason
with the paradox of shame?
I called you many times
but you always changed your name.

I told you everything
but you said I lied.
I cleansed myself with water
but swam against the tide,
trying to find a reason
why Christ was crucified.

The path to darkness
was written and scored
we waited for centuries
both the rich and the poor
with promises of change
we'd already heard before.

Redemption is spent
by those richer than me
who try to predict
what they can't even see
and then make you pay
for what should really be free.

Barefoot dancers on a
sea of glass

turn the pages back
to the past
forever is a word
that rarely seems to last.

Giancarlo Moruzzi

Willow

The Willow bends
the Willow sways
sat by the river
counting the days
guarding the silence
like a brave silent knight
rattling his leaves
to the bird's delight.

Giancarlo Moruzzi

Desperate Hours

Locked inside
a wireless prison
darkness steals the pages
from the feral light of dusk,
rifling through her followers
to see who she can trust.
Lupine in her insincerity
she kneels to greet
the Autumn's song.
Her oral calligraphy
veined in perfection.
She breaths in slow whispers
confined by the movement
of her desperate hours.

Giancarlo Moruzzi

The Warrior

The warrior waited
dressed in darkness
shouldering his cold arrows of death.
Fostered from Roman Gods,
threatened by sleep
he watches paths of glory
lined up in front of him,
like loneliness.
He carries his penance
like a victory
while tears run down his cheek
like a false baptism.
In this soulless cluster
of space
he came to regret
the inevitable,
while kneeling upon burning cinders
to ask for release.
In his sphere of darkness
he waits for the highest bidder.
In a market of thieves
he still manages to smile.

Giancarlo Moruzzi

Fate Foretold

Ashen Princess
draped in gold splinters
ambles between spires and spells.
A fate foretold,
she will experience pain
like never before.
Flowers placed on remnants
of the past
that were kept alive for too long.
Bare fingers stripped
by the nights silence,
write in a strange calligraphy.
Tears wept in vain
you came to touch
the troubled water
where sailors
were once the new God's,
sailing away on salty ships
time was their destiny.
Prophecies fulfilled
In uncertain climates.
Sanctuary sought in loose asylums
while the wilderness summoned
it's tired sisters back
for one last call to arms.

Giancarlo Moruzzi

Push the Plough - preamble

As we struggle to feed our growing population, worldwide farming practices have become more aggressive. Crop monocultures, animal breeding, herbicides, insecticides, fertilizers: all taking a lasting toll on the ground and the ecology.

This lyric is taken from the new album by Pagan Harvest. www.pagenharvest.com

Push the Plough

    Push the plough.

Aim the beam and plough the furrow.
Soft grain, heavy rain.
Grind the seed until tomorrow.
All pain for sons of Cain.

    Push the earth.
    Plough the earth.
    Rape the earth.

Mutilate the natural order.
Strange beasts strange fodder.
Mutant mammals, fitter, harder.
Meat feasts, sick larder.

Grey-green leaves unfurling.
Spring's bright signal signed.

All the heavens circling,
To the earth they tie and bind.

Turn to light.
Sacred solar union.
Heliotrope rite.
Curious spring communion.

    Push the plough.

Harvest all of autumn's bounty.
Fill the barns, hoard the crops.
Dry and cure and pickle plenty.
Winter yawns never stops.

    Push the earth.
    Plough the earth.
    Rape the earth.

Push our planet to the limit.
Alien wind, chemical rain.
We have all just gone insane.
Solar flares come again.

Distant leafless branches
fuse to grey-brown haze.
Rotting leaves discarded
regenerate and so amaze

Genetic crops.
Fruits enlarging.

Acid drops.
Phosphates charging.

>Push the earth.
>Plough the earth.
>Rape the earth.

Lawrence Reed

My Body's A Temple Part 1: Pill

      Pills, pills, confounded pills.
So many pills in these silly chemical times.
So many pills to keep at bay so many ills.
Blue pills to excite.
Delightful yellow pills, bright orange pills.
But pills are nearly aways white.
Medicine's benign blight.

Statins mark the three-lettered days
with fourteen pricks of the two-week pack
and keep more thick blood flowing back
without a cholesterol-induced heart attack.
Haemoglobin roving to the brain's grey core
like homeopathic smack.

Then the small blue miracle
that keeps the pecker up to muck about
and drill and bore and surge and spout.
Fulfil the ambition and end the drought.
Roll me fucking over in the four-leafed fucking clover!
While other pills kill that roaring urge
and screw my body-temple royally over.

      Pills, pills, sodding pills.
Antibiotics for the boring long-haul bugs.
Amoxicillin, ciprofloxacin, azithromycin.
A triad of great ancient gods.
Pills to still my stuttering heart
and ease my groggy body snuggling to sleep.

Pills (or illicit drugs?) to speed me up
for greater thrills and spills.

Naproxen for that potent edge,
slicing through the sciatica scream.
No-frills paracetamol pills
for pains and colds and flu and chills.

    Pills, pills, pissing pills.
Cabinet closeted.
An unforgiving hissing fluorescent strip.
And a senseless mirror.

Willy-nilly pre-emptive pills.
Herbal voodoo stuff that instils bad luck
and make me shiver.
Multivitamin pills to stop the biological hoodoo.
Milk thistle and B12 for the booze-soaked,
star-struck liver.

    Pills, pills, accursed pills.
Pills that purge like leaches, drawing juices still.
Allopurinol to dilute the uric acid that stirs the gout.
               Pills to dilute you.
               Until. . . Full stop. Over and out.
               Phew!

Lawrence Reed

Excerpt 10 from the epic poem The Barricade - *out of body moment number 3. Dealing with the extraordinary smells I encountered in a 1984 pub.*

My out-of-body moment #3

Olfactory systems have been overloaded to breaking so far;
odour distinctions killed in this heady bouquet-de-bar.
Now, sudden nostril fracture:
all the elements are singularly distilled
by the master perfumer,
ready to savour and smell.
My nose is over-filled
with heaven's scents and hell's malodours;
all heaven-sent.

Hag parfum-hum:
Hairy Mary's Beautiful,
    Salome's Poison,
        Mary M's Paris.
Blokes' sharp cheap fragrances:
piercing 'brutal' aftershaves of the Billingsgate boys;
other Punters' Old Spice;
Luke's Obsession For Men.
The smack of deodorants and tacky talcs
for armpits and nether places.
Sweat reeking from the underarm-stained spray-
abstained.

Antiseptic haemorrhoid bum-cream. (Mm Germolene.)
Vick chest-rub.
Faint Savlon taint.

A hint of ethereal, menthol cigarette floats,
Bensons, Players No 6 and Marlboro fill the middle notes.
Some duty-free Gauloises and Gitanes lends novel heft;
nuanced by the piling trays of butts and penitents' ash;
just left.
Heavier yet, raw tobacco:
roll-your-owns and ripe bonfire pipes;
tar traces from trendy cigarillos
and a sad, nipple-sucked cigar.
Woodsmoke and bold coal aroma
add the massive symphonic basso profundo.

Soaked bitch Vicky in heat.

Cheap whisky and brandy fumes,
stale beers, modish brews.
Wines in stages of secondary fermentation sourness.
Rum 'n' toxic Coke.
Scottish peat and French oak.
Hints of gin and herby Italian vermouth.
Salt and malt vinegar, cheese and onion.
Bogus beef: sacrificial twiglets.
Dry-roasted farty nuts.
Unclean roasted pig's skin: crackling.
(Split hoof but does not chew the cud.)
Eggs in acetic acid.

The noxious, mildewed Gents.

*Aggressive ammoniacal cleaner fluid,
acrid pear-drops and waxy polish.
Brasso, and methanol mirror cleanser.
Dirty, soapy, mop and bucket.
Bar towels soaked in the varied Side One fluids.*

*Jackets with historic puke stains
supporting their own ecosystems.*

*Fetor of breath from a legion of devil's angels,
topped by the savour of the Billingsgate boys'
special umami-humming vibe:
J&J's lingering anchovy burps.
Bart's and a few others' fragrant guffy farts.*

The foul fug of the Mugs' Tap Room.

*Effluvia from all usual bodily excretions
from orifices and moist skin,
with a few mysterious tangs thrown in
from both sexes.*

Definite whiff of eau-de-toilet.

Quintessential bouquet: crutch-sprayed trousers.

It's really too much.

Then...

A rarefied untainted draught beckons me

to resume my quest with renewed vigilance...

Lawrence Reed

Excerpt 11 from the epic poem The Barricade- *the Thirteen Emblems. Do you remember Thirteen Profane Emblems from earlier editions? Here they are examined in more detail.*

_____ **Station XI - Nailing** and valedictory orders.

I'm desperate to unknot meaning in the metamorphosis, while dawdling through **Side Two.** Then my axes get revised. In the lengthy eleventh hour the thirteen emblems appear atomised. Cleaved apart by my 'water-rat's' slashing cutlass. Rattling my glassy eyes. Draining things of vitality with my exhaustive gaze. Squeezing out the essence. Capturing and amassing sharper detail with razor-cut singular form.
Ciphers setting fiddly riddles. Hatching out.
Sending animation signs.
Sprouting divergent byzantine natures;
assuming viable vital entities of their own shrewd designs.
Each a critical component entwined in this grubby shrine.
There is a well-worn city-synchronicity
as these crude human and inanimate forms align.
Recombining with fine sibylline serendipity.
I refocus on the event-horizon
       as the thirteen emblems revitalize and revive. . .

(i) Sepia stools, tripod-steady, stony-hard.
(Unlike the dodgy stools in the blokes' bog.)
Legs go church-pew numb.

(ii) Hazel seats, harder still, freezing bums both fat and bony.
Punters wriggle and squirm for a little blood flow,
wearing bare the boot-brown varnish below.

(iii) Tarnished tables lie too low,
grazing Punter's thighs and knobbly knees.
Prone to rise expectantly in exciting hijinks phases;
during the wild Cribb, three-card brag, and domino sprees.
Whoopee!
Some hide arcane machinery from a bygone Victorian manufactory,
raison d'être lost; purposelessly free.

(iv) The parliament of Punters poses statuesque,
gothic hard-carved, tainted saints;
worn, with peeling paint; no regrets, no complaints.
A flaky front-row massive. Earnest and forlorn inebriants.
Dragging on carcinoma-cigs, draining hepatoma-kegs.
Morose, broad, lacerated; broken Darwinian links.
Still, always a charitable cheeky clink:
"Cheers big ears." Guts groan and flop. Jowls sink.

(v) Bit by bit more bawdy herds of heathen Hags convene.
Not exactly mutton, nor lamb,
but sitting somewhere succulent and a little tough in between.
The Hags in the Saloon Bar usually hit the cryptic holy ratio of one to seven dicks:
vital to this slick outfit's functioning.

Cosmic strings are getting stretched to breaking point
in a universe expanding so fast.
Like the knicker elastic getting a workout on the dancefloor.

Handbags tucked under armpits like symbolic broomsticks.

The Stones are pumping Start Me Up (inducing sexy, rhythmic, pubic fits).
These skanks *could* make a dead man come. (The pits, but I truly believe it.)
Powder-puffs open for a titillating daubing (filling epidermal slits).
Lipstick tips extended; prophetic symbol. (Getting pornographic.)
Marginally sagging tits (a tell-tale token beneath their clinging habits).
Slurping with cannibalistic appetite:
Sweet Martini (Italian chic);
Campari (Luton airport super-chic);
Bacardi rum with 'the real thing!' (doing their island ting);
Babycham (the risqué 'leg-opener');
G 'n' T with a slice and two knobs. . . of ice. (Ooh la la! Nice);
faint-tinted Mateus Rosé ('no way Jose');
Blue Nun (catering for the more Catholic taste of Mary M).

Swarming clouds of some mystifying small-fly species are sugar-seduced,
creating a tranquillised grey aura;
gradually reduced as they're engulfed in the barflies' sickly libations.
These crass barfy lasses still swill away their elation-passes,
downing Punter-paid refilled glasses,
oblivious to the drowning Diptera masses.

Wines transmogrified from base water
re-enact Christ's classy first miracle,

with the bitter-sweet foretaste of his execution by station
twelve.
Tainted Love comes temptingly on, the vinyl revolves,
stoking desires to turn cartwheels and prance.
Hags: bleeding, gushing and leeching, jukebox-entranced,
advance to their improvised dancefloor and adopt their stance.
Crushed into their eccentric, mushy, Canaan wedding-dance;
hips gyrate, booties shake, years peel away.
The audience does more than glance!
Pendulous boobs swing, undulate and nearly rotate.
There's a titillating rush of high-octane romance.
Slushy sex awaits these scrumptious Eves.
The lushes' cheeks erotically flush cerise.
Sweet Jesus!
No touching. . . please I cannot stand the way they tease!
(Mary M and Salome very pleasing.)

Waning cuties, pert to pudgy booty,
floating too serenely to Little Richard:
performing their angelic duty like a cloud of puffed-up puttis
about to auger some profound sacrifice or birth of a new age.
Tutti-frutti!
    Nice.
        Aw rooty!

Camouflaged with expertly plastered facial crags,
clothed in close-fitting racy glad-rags.
Crowning glory: stocking-snags.
The prescient Hags slyly eye-up their predestined slithery shags.
War paint fades on this messy, sedated, shop-worn horde,
belying their coming ascendant parade.

The Saracen-Punters' powers of resistance fade
with the coven's imminent raids.
Brandishing inverted hearts as weapons of war: spades!
Rebelling, reborn, to perform dry-eyed masterclasses.
Like the whip-hand Warrior Women of medieval Crusades:
weapons, subtle and whetted; cunning war-cries;
they are sworn to rise and never fail,
have their gory glorious hour; seize the prized, blooded, Holy Grail.
Canonized.
Their boggling powers will always surprise,
viewed through the frail Punters' sozzled, beer-goggle eyes.

(vi) Mugs in exile institute a partisan breakaway band of sub-subalterns,
slithering like slugs to-and-fro in a nebulous, formless, smoky patio-Arcadia.
Slime spirals and trails define the path's design. It' not good.
A diaspora of disbarred advocates with no homeland, no sheltering,
crammed in their moonlit fag-incense temple to Pan; banned from indoors.
Banned from even Public Bar life.
Pathetic putrid seeds, sowed by the bad, calloused hands
of a faceless hooded sower on barren, arid, land.
Sad destinies and deeds dispassionately planned.
Stunted roots, no foothold between rocks and sand.
Choked by vigorous thorns and weeds.
Craving Ve's sympathetic deed of constant 'watering' to be freed;
a pandering only afforded those already damned.

Slavering slaves; dog-brains on high-wire alert.
Blathering, hand in glove, in unintelligible tongues of fire.
Trying to intercede. Stoking their pyre.
Ablaze with loveless passion
on their peculiar Pentecostal planet of grief and pain.
Gazing at Zion, a distant, hazy hill-city,
beyond reach for these caned, outcast Sons of Cain.
Crazy paving floods as the spectral Euphrates
and Tigris rivers rage and amaze.
A calm mournful Psalmody floats from the music-box:
by the rivers of Babylon, there we sat down, yea we wept.

The Mugs chant their own primitive unsung psalm in modal tones
to any deity, or any sentient thing,
that may hear their godforsaken race.
Plangent, guttural, mantra-like groans.
In return these loners receive sod all, not even the faintest rumour of grace.

(vii) The Gents' reek concentrates minute by minute;
stale piss mixed with fetid sloppy shit. No signed exit.
A runny, miasmic monument for dogged determination not to quit
among any poor doomed souls braving this diabolical pit.

(viii) The dartboard swells where it's been over-hit,
around the fives and ones, and bunghole bit,
by arrows miss-aimed, because, so the Punter's say, it's badly lit.
(We all know, like the pool, they are basically just shit.
(ix) Staccato clicks and spasmodic knocks

come slinking in from a cool, dim backroom annex,
home to hot-headed phases of pickled-prick pool.
Pool cues studiously racked and stacked by some sagacious curator
like an ancient spear display from an historic battle.
Young Punters, getting shirty, duel with the cruel crooked sticks.
Balls move in Brownian motion across crinkled, azure baize
as dazed double-vision rules.
Amazed and bored, the pool-Punters' entropy eventually decays.

(x) The spluttering fire burns soggy logs and spits
on to poor old Vicky.
(Remember Manky James's dispirited, dozing liver-and-black dog?)
She yelps a rabid shriek and jerks as if speared, poor crossbred bitch,
straining her frayed leash tied around a fender,
which softly splits.
She limps off to the Public Bar
in the hopeless hope of some Mugs' affection and crispy tit-bits.

(xi) The mirror's reflected past returns in inane, infidel, fizzing fits.
A boundless reservoir of all that has ever happened in this room.
Fate whizzing by, much too fast. Wait, wait, wait!
White Rabbit berates his chained fob-watch. Late, late, late!
Ten chuffing minutes late for a 'very important date'.
Following the wise bunny, down the funny rabbit hole. . .
boozy memories ooze; muddling Mary's fragmentary Jesus lies.
Befuddling, like the ever-buzzing bar-flies.

(xii) The one-armed-bandit's curses bind.
Erratic electric algorithms, flashing fruity lights, random sounds.
Jinxed predestination as the priapic chrome handle is jerked.
"Huuurgh!"
The hoodoo bandit fruit revolves,
the spellbound Punter's cash floods
into the well of its voodoo spell.
The Ants bash their double-drum, jungle rhythms.
Adam sings Stand And Deliver! The wheels grind.
Eden's rotten fruit unkindly unwinds,
robbing mindless, star-crossed desperados blind.
Your money or your life.
No 'monkey' jackpot clunk, no ker-chunk-ker-chunk
for the luckless, ant-brained, feckless drunk.

(xiii) The jukebox fluoresces; undefinable pseudo-pastel shades
from an unworldly rainbow arched on some distant moon.
Flicking, combing, interchanging.
Doing their own sublime dance, aside to the music,
at their own pulse and vibe,
hypnotically merging under the blurry Perspex
into one colour unknown to external nature.
I pay the box's quid fine and take a gander at the vinyl
(ethanol's cousin chemical).
Some stock knees-up 'forty-fives' evoke lives of past decades.
So, I repeat the shit old Bach-organ hit:
baroque seventeen-thirty meets. . . 'The Summer of Lurve'.
Bach's geometric lines pedantically bent and bowed
by the billowing Hammond organ's swell.
Orchestral suite number three: BWV one zero six eight (don't ya know).

An elegant air, lost on the three G-stringed Hags with no lines visible below.
N. V. P. bums looking great though. . . 'five six seven eight. . . step and. . . go. . .'
We turn a whiter shade of pale
as the trio skips a jukebox-approximate light fandango,
jangling desperately to the jagged counterpoint.
Orbiting the triangle of handbags
like rum-drunk pirates around a treasure hoard,
or devil worshipers
forming some occult arrangement to conjure the Lord of the Flies:
Blessed Mary's classy Gucci;
glistening in the pub's glow, Salome's Chanel Gold Chain Classic Flap
(double interlocked Cs);
and Mary Mag's Louis Vuitton Bucket Bag (good for emergency vomit).
Bragging bag-brands with one snag: ersatz, like the Hags.
Cunning Camden Market knock-offs that won't see out the year.
Hypnotic, slaggy moves. Hips gyrate in simulated shagging.
Glasses in one hand, in the other long-ashed fags.
Gamma-aminobutyric acid courses. . . 'GABA' hits; reduced inhibitions take hold.

A time to mourn, and a time to dance. Alleluia!

Next up: Dancing Queen's enticing strains put the Hags in heat!
Bang on the beat.
They dance and weave, and on they dance, through the agony of the high-heel pain,

threading about the handbag pile, the Three Graces cast in thongs,
encircling ruinous classical remains.
We all open our strong hearts and let the thumping music flow in.
Blasting far too blasted loud, for Abba Father's sake.
Too long, for Christ's sake.
So wrong, crap song, 'gets my goat'.
But nobody complains; The Holy Spirit reigns.
We all feel we belong.
Bjorn again!
Evensong, pure-form for this throaty throng singing along.
It totally 'floats our boats'.
'Ding dong.'
We're having the time of our lives.
What could possibly go wrong?

> Thirteen profane Side Two emblems all accounted for.
> Bong. . .

Lawrence Reed

If Not, Then Why Not?

Your leisure is your prose
Your work is your poetry
Losing the will to live

Conceding points of order
Naked self wants to clothe
Clothed self needs to disrobe

Made beds to contemplate
To stalk around your room
Moments utterly corrupted

This music isn't helpful
This place isn't uplifting
This mood is persistent

Romanticism leads to cumulative fatigue
Complex natures shun birth
First name terms are ferocious

Days are against conquering you
Made better by seeing you
Annihilated less than a year ago

And no sooner are you done
You begin to assimilate another
You must be apart from this

Every sounds crashes like thunder
Increasing care is taken
Impulses improve with a lack of feeling

Your eyes have opened a little
It's essential to see the universe
Its attraction is what you live for

And who among us isn't lonely?
And why among us doesn't fear humanity?
And who among us doesn't recoil?

Not all pain is psychosomatic
Not all miracles lead to torment
Not all concern is feminine

Interludes include beclouding
Unbearable is the most awful when leaving
Too many dangerous things happen

You're held in high regard
Artistic as your ideals are essential
More to be damned than pitied

If you ever read this
If you ever speak out loud
If you ever say yes to adoration

Which is to say in season
Reserve the right to spring forward
Onward to a purer moonlit finish

And yet you've grown
Because myths sleep with whores
It matters little to you

What nonsense the wolf howls
Can't stand schedules any longer
You have the physical strength to endure it

Openings to remind you
Signatures of a dozen tired faces
You merge into many personalities

Increasingly difficult as it has become
Acquaintances long since perished
Following questions with core questions

And in trying to find work
You constantly analyse neurosis
These toys are ugly and expensive

Almost everything at risk
Avail yourself to unwrapped parcels
Become sick about these moments

Can't stomach criticism
Can't stomach more arguments
Can't stomach how others live

Medicate rather than resume
Fail as fast and as far as you can
Spend your eternity sightseeing

Fall in love with your divorced self
These diversions are continuing
Encounters growing increasingly tempestuous

By the time you return
Excitement has been cashed in
Airbrushed and made quite envious

This may be the best thing for you
This may lead to happiness
This may project your guilt complex

Just admire at arm's length
You've so much more to do
Absorb the people shouting

Your pleasure is for someone else
Your hormones are your current
Rock gently against muddled pricks

Act out of sympathy
Cannot be annoyed lately
Cede to passion unconsciously

Much later or the next morning
Disappointment dies in wonder
Love's labour is synchronised

No words address the pregnant pause
Bureaucratic worlds feast unsparingly
Intelligence falls short of thinking

Fanatics and real liberals are everywhere
Materialism is most vulgar today
Every generation is dragged around

You do not want to be absurd
You do not want to be undecided
You do not want to be officially engaged

Once sober inebriation waits
All you've gained is distorted
Serving discouragement

Resent at leisure simultaneous fixes
Miscellaneous tricks convince you of this
Nothing more bizarre than living

Your future is permanently nearer
Partying with fiasco
Flirting with disaster

Can't connect or hold on
Laughter is the same as frowning
Stricter methods are indulgent

Be unorthodox as you suggest
Mention honesty as progress
Unless you're kind to everyone

Amorphous limits you discover
Move to a different rhythm
Anything to crown a high point

Estimate your emotional anger
Stay at home less dimly
Your dreams are an immediate escape

Weighed down by a load of stuff
You loathe regret's return
You rule the madhouse

It only takes one bloodrush
Attractively thrown before being snatched away
No one curious enough to assuage your falsity

Somehow fun eludes you
It earns but cannot spend
It addresses the party in your absence

Must you be drugged to be creative?
Must you sit in the presence of beauty?
Must you grow thinner by the minute?

You try to keep your light touch alive
It drifts to smother sensuality
Say goodnight to tomb ballet.

Meek

A Weary World

What is the future?
It all seems so bleak,
It's the clock,
Tick-ticking
To a Third World War,
What is our fate?
With all this hate,
With so much chaos,
The Congress is cat and mouse,
They pass no laws,
They are full of flaws,
Unrest and uncertainty is everywhere
People are full of fear,
What is the future?
It all seems so bleak,
It's the clock,
Tick-ticking
To a Third World War,
God help us all!

Celine Rose Mariotti

Faces Of Yesteryear

It seems a lifetime ago,
Those Happy Faces on our TV screen,
Those Faces of Yesteryear,
People like Shirley Booth
Who played "Hazel"
Hazel's love for people
and for life,
her good-natured spirit
Mr. B. depended on her,
and she always freely gave her advice,
Stories on TV nowadays have no love,
No spirit, no common decency,
No storyline
The Faces of Yesteryear
How long ago it seems,
You'd turn on the Evening News
With Walter Cronkite
He was the epitome of what a newsman should be,
He reported the news of the day,
He was sophisticated with perfect diction,
and had command and knowledge of the
current events of the day
He always signed off on his broadcast,
"And that's the way it is, and then he'd say the date,"
November 22, 1963 (the day President Kennedy was shot)
He is etched in American TV history forever,
Faces of Yesteryear
They sing in our hearts forever,
Like the one and only Dean Martin
Every Thursday night on his TV show on NBC,

He'd slide down the poll,
Always sang so relaxed,
My grandfather always said Dean made it look so easy,
The way he sang, because he was so relaxed,
Everyone enjoyed Dean,
My Dad was a big fan of Dean Martin,
His music lives on forever,
"You're Nobody Till Somebody Loves You";
"Everybody Loves Somebody Sometime";
"Send Me the Pillow";
"Remember Me, I'm the One Who Loves You";
"An Evening in Roma"; "Houston"
"I Will"; "Chapel in the Moonlight"
And many, many, many more
We will all remember "The Dean Martin Roast,"
He'd roast a celebrity,
And the guest stars would do a comedy routine,
Some of those guest stars were:
Ruth Buzzi, Foster Brooks, Don Rickles,
Milton Berle, Rich Little and many more,
Great entertainment for all,
Yes, the Faces of Yesteryear,
How long ago,
But we'll always treasure,
We'll always remember,
Those Faces of Yesteryear.

Celine Rose Mariotti

A Musical Bear

There he is
My musical bear
He sings such sweet songs,
His music fills the air,

There he is
My musical bear
His songs are rock n roll,
He brings so much cheer,

There he is
My musical bear
Coming to me with a big hug,
He is such a dear,

There he is
My musical bear
He sings such sweet songs,
His music fills the air.

Celine Rose Mariotti

Somewhere Long, Long Ago

All those years gone by,
So many tears to cry,
We're back to the early 1900's,
The time of World War One,
They too had a Pandemic,

The Influenza,
So many dead from the war,
Their bodies buried in Flanders Field
American cemetery,
Where the poppies grow,

In the country of Belgium,
People in the US lost their lives,
To the Pandemic
From 1918-1919,
Woodrow Wilson was President,

The Treaty of Versailles was signed,
World War I was over,
President Wilson delivered
The Treaty to the Senate,
First President since 1789

To deliver a treaty to the US Senate,
He formed the League of Nations,
Soon, the Influenza
That took so many lives
Was over too

Life started anew,
The Roaring 20's began,
The pain and loss of World War I
And the Influenza
Soon began to fade . . .

Celine Rose Mariotti

Skinny, I Miss You So
Skinny (My Dad),
Our affectionate name for him

He was a special person in our lives,
always the one to help us out,
to run an errand,
to bring the mail to the Post Office,
to help make the beds in the morning,
to take my Mom to the doctor
or hairdresser

When I was a kid,
He'd take me to Banko's
for my guitar lessons,
He'd take me for my blood tests,
We'd watch the New York Giants
together,

We'd all go to the Oakdale Theater
in Wallingford to see a concert,
The first one we went to in 1976,
was Tom Jones
My sister and I took a picture with
him on stage

My Dad would help us fold the
Newsletters for our Tom Terrific
Tom Jones Fan Club
Our Dad Skinny always there for us

Not a day goes by
We don't talk about him,
Skinny, I miss you so.

Celine Rose Mariotti

My Cup Overfloweth

We all have our crosses
To bear
And in our own unique ways
Shoulder.
My cup overfloweth.
Drenches and spills.
How best to drink
The many to gulp?

Going through it as automaton
Day by day
Hour by hour and even...minute by minute
Like the fly on the wall
Looking on.

The well of emotions stir
That impostor feeling -
Belonging to someone else.
Dared to have stolen,
This is someone else's ache.
Yet, in the hidden
Shadow,
Unfurled and
Gazed upon -
Caught the breath
And stung the eye
Tugged the heart
And flooded the brain.
Then, with swift rebuke

Emotions are scolded back to their shadows
To drift into the dark unlit abyss.

And whilst the body
Cannot hide
Nor conceal
That which
The poisons wreak,
The spirit's soul,
Ever taking by surprise,
Stalwartly,
Reaches down into the shadows
And with illuminating hand
Lends a solacement.
To my overfloweth cup.

Niamh Mahon.

Putting The Laundry Away

Putting the laundry away
Pondering on knickers.
No longer white
But grey from all the washing.
Should the folded pairs be
Put away in the drawer,
Dyed or thrown away?

Throw those old knickers out
They are old and grey.
No, there is good wear left in them!
Think of the planet.
Nobody sees them.
Nobody but you.
Your time is done
Carry on
Make do
Slipper shuffle.
Those days are gone
Gone forever,
Put the kettle on.

Dye them then!
They'll look better...
On the clothesline.
Just a little care
Like the hair
Dyed?
They won't look grey!
Nor old, nor shabby,

Nor new.
Make do,
Re-use, recycle
Re.... deuce!
No win, no lose.
No tatty embarrassment...
...If seen.

Or throw them away,
Sling them,
Fling them.
Buy new...
Knickers.
Worth it
It is about you.
Self-worth
Seen or not seen
Irrelevant.
How they make you feel?
What is underneath?

Knickers...!

Niamh Mahon.

The Little Things

It's the little things that matter...
They are a switch, a gateway, a trigger...
A bolt out of the blue –
Out of nowhere –
Unexpected
The straw that breaks
The little things
Shouldered
Managed
Heroically
Stoically
Just got on with.
It is the little things nevertheless,
The little things
That stop your heart
Hold your breath
Smart your eyes
Stir the emotions.
The little things.
The little things, the little ones...
Like suddenly noticing
Cheese grated finely on the plate
Flash!
The way the little one liked it,
On the side and never on top
Flash!
His brother munching
A whole red peppers
Flash!
Their Mum's baby teeth marks

In the cucumber returned to the fridge.
The little things, the little ones
Swiftly, unexpectedly
Transported back in time
From the back of my mind
Where sweet memories hide
From fear of hurt.
It's the little things,
The little things that grow
Day by day
Even out of sight or
Out of conscious mind
The little ones grow
And grow
Without me there
Without a role
Without a presence
Without...
It's the little things,
The little ones.

Niamh Mahon.

Mouse

So, there I am standing in my kitchen, my nice clean, sanitised, tidy kitchen, WhatsApping away while the supper cooks. It is a simple supper, which I may not even eat, but who knows, an appetite may come to me, if not, I can plate it an pop it in the fridge for tomorrow. The WhatsApp conversations are welcome, they are with my two Goddaughters - they are making me laugh and raising my spirits – love those girls!

I am in the corner of the kitchen, elbow on the work surface, fingers busy, eyes scanning, mind engaged, when something breaks the engagement. I lift my head out of the messages and look to the opposite side of the kitchen to below the far cupboard. I hold my gaze for a moment, and then scan the area... nothing. Then back to the messages. Again, something in the corner of my eye pulls my attention away. This time, my eyes widen in surprise! It is a small pointy head with glassy eyes and twitching whiskers, poking from under the cupboard door!

"Oh no! Not a mouse in the cupboard, not in that cupboard, not **that** cupboard," occupied my thoughts for a split second. The cupboard that houses all the occasional use equipment, tins, bowls, jugs etc... No NOT THAT cupboard! The mind fast forwards to the potential task ahead.... It will take forever to empty, wash and disinfect the contents of that cupboard... my knees will aches with the kneeling and bending – and there is my back. The place will be a mess; it will take an age, bloody cat! Brining in a mouse. Then, the mind swiftly shifts into reverse gear and...

"So, that is what that noise was all about last night!"

The cat brought in a mouse and this one was a feisty one, it got away and hid. But why in that cupboard? Well, that explains why the cat's bed was in the middle of the dinning-room rather than in its usual place, the corner. Hmm, it really did give the cat a run for her money! Good on you mouse, good on you.

And then the spilt second was over, and I was still glaring at the mouse's poking head. Then it emerged further into the room...not far, 30 cm or so...then retreating ...then back out and retreating then back out... I stood still watching... then a retreat back into the cupboard.

By this time, a plan was made: open the cupboard door, open the kitchen door that leads to the yard and wait, watch...stay and make sure it really does go out...

Without, pause, the plan is actioned, and I waited. And not in vain, within moments the beastie was poking out again, but this time, it wasn't from the cupboard, it was from over the kickboard under the cupboard! Happy days! No, trawling through the contents of THAT cupboard.

Out it came tentatively, 20 cm, then 30 cm then 40 cm along the edge of the kickboards, then back then forward, then back and then forward...and I held my pose still and waited...willing it to move towards the open door and vacate the kitchen. I took a photo to share with the Goddaughters and WhatsApped them with the news. This was one healthy looking, silky furred rodent with a twinkle in its eye. Then, it changed direction, it saw me, well it must have. It came toward me, I held my position, it came closer... closer right up to my slippers. Looking down, I saw the mouse to my right, the cat food bowl to my left and my feet in their slippers betwixt the two!

Again, the mind zapped a thought...so that is why the cat's food has been disappearing so quickly – I had wondered if the cat was getting lazy, greedy, overeating – I'd been refilling her bowl more often than usual... now I knew why. This mouse is living here... behind the kickboard? No. Really could it be? No! Then, as it went to traverse over my slipper, I raise my foot and it darted back to it gap over the kickboard and disappeared.

I thought it gone for the night, when out it poked again... this time it skirted along the kickboard to the far end of the kitchen towards the open door. Great!

"Good, go little mouse, go, escape...keep going...keep going." And on it continued, until it met the cat's water bowl. It didn't go around it; it slunk right up into the water bowl and drank!

"What, are you having a laugh? You cheeky little ... you bloody live here...you have food you have water, you have warmth and now a nest probably behind the kickboard... A NEST!!! What babies? More mice...NOOO!!"

Maybe not yet, maybe it is just setting up, getting ready, yes it did look fat. Did it? Maybe no babies yet. With this thought in my head I reached for the soft brush – I will help it out – help it to leave - help it out the door! It scurried up to the door frame, ran along in and back again and back along the open door frame.

"Go on, out...go on... out!"

With brush in hand, I scooped at the rodent, but it was too fast for me, it dodged each attempt to swoosh it out. A scurry between occurred – electric with action and excitement until it disappeared over and behind the kickboard at the far end of the kitchen.

It has not been seen since.
Where was the cat during all this? Watching TV...

The cat slept in the kitchen for the next few nights. However, there has been no more evidence of the mouse. The food and water was removed. No sounds, no mice faeces, no interest from the cat. Nothing.

Niamh Mahon.

Catalonian Roadside Poppies

Malnourished young women, impossibly thin,
in croptops, and g-strings or skinny blue jeans.
working girls - literally - children
promising heaven to middle aged men

on the side of the road

they strike their pose
(an internationally recognized code)
that seems to say, 'if you pay,
anything goes'

brightly coloured parasols
like poppies decorating the side of the road,
mark the spots where their sex is sold
in clearings cut into bamboo groves.

or is it sugar cane
in this part of spain
where the drivers take a break
from their working day?

but how little do these men pay?

for

fucking
sucking
pushing
pulling

belly flapping
stroking
slapping

petting
licking
groping
poking

drooling
groaning
grunting
coming

crying
pining
mewling
spewing

spitting
splitting
bleeding
pleading

patting
tapping
pissing
crapping
wheezing
groaning
eyeballs rolling

how little do they pay
before they get on their way
to iron out the details
of a sale they've just made?

muttering something about currency exchange
or a delivery delay - it's just another working day

and the girls?

what price do they pay?
when they just do it

again

        and again

                and again.

Richard Earls.

Your Halo's Slipping

Your use of personal contacts
Your interest in professional success
Your lack of a current itinerary
Your reflected diary location
Your pathetic crossing of borders
Your persistent fear of literary giants
Your cooling of passionate affairs
Your aptly titled publications
Your contemptuous take on world politics
Your self-doubt mired in sudden swoops
Your happy endings found in books
Your disgraceful conduct reverberates
Your oiled wings learning to fly
Your shame given its rightful name
Your absurdity in bless yourself
Your sexual drive at low ebb
Your grey energy taking to the air
Your atmosphere so dense that it hurts
Your last word in a fuzzy manner
Even your staunchest critics stand in awe.

Meek

Bullies

Look at me am big and strong
Can beat up anyone who does me wrong
Now there are times when the innocent one
Weak and scared along they come

This is my chance to prove to you
I can show you just what I can do
Torment put fear into you all
I will always win I'll never fall

You see my gang all cheer me on
This gives me Power to prove I'm strong
But wait you BULLIES come on your own
With no back up you stand alone

Against your victims what have they to lose
Nothing for you have tortured and abused
Made them feel there's nowhere to run
Well I'm afraid to say it's now your turn

To be afraid now you try to run
Your victims now stand one by one
But where's your gang? There's no one here
You alone can you feel the fear

I hope you can for one day this will come
Karma will get you and then you'll be the one
Scared afraid now how will you feel
Bullying is Torture the fear is real

Power is US your victims we win
For you stand alone when the fight does begin
You see the world stands by us the ones who are weak
(But are we really?) Let the world speak.

Heather Snedden

Authors:

Robyn Isobel Florence McEwan: I am 12 years old. I have autism.

Celine Rose Mariotti: Celine Rose Mariotti is an accomplished writer whose work has appeared in magazines all over the USA, Canada, England, Scotland, Australia and India. Some of those magazines include: Night Roses, Green's Magazine, Poet's Review, Poet's Art, Tombigbee, Offerings, Poets at Work, Hindu Young World, Magnolia Quarterly, Lone Stars Magazine, Poetsespresso, Artifacts, Quantum Leap, Frost Fire Worlds, Children's Magazine of India, Tigershark Publishing, Atlantean Publishing, Pink Chameleon, FreeXpression, Northern Stars Magazine, Creative Inspirations, Utopia Science Fiction Magazine, Poesis, Rainy Day Poems, and many more. Bewildering Stories has accepted some of her poems for publication and Shemom has accepted two of her poems. Altered Reality Magazine has published several of her poems. She has had several books published. The books are: "Olivia MacAllister, Who Are You?" Another book is "I'm Too Young to be President" published by Clayborn Press of AZ. "Leapy the Frog" was published by Magbooks of HongKong. WriteWords.com published "I Have a Friend on Jupiter"; "Minister's Shoes" and "Minister's Corporate Escapades." And some other books she self-published: "Through Celine's Eyes", "Words of Inspiration" "Red, White and Blue", all poetry books and a nonfiction book, "What Corporate America is Really All About". She has also self-published "I Hear The Banjo Playing", a ghost story. Her newest book is "The Return of George Bowman", sequel to "I Hear the Banjo Playing". Hierath Publishing has published her book "Atomic Soldiers". He has also accepted her other two books-"Out There in Space" and "The Rebellion". Celine has a B.S. degree in Business Administration with a minor in English from Sacred Heart University in Fairfield, CT. She plays the guitar and banjo; has her own home business, CRM Enterprises and her own online newsletter she publishes. She lives with her family in Shelton, CT. She loves Las Vegas and she loves to watch the soap operas.

Patricia Bell: My name is Patricia Bell. I am a retired teacher with responsibility for Special Needs. I've written Children's stories for years as a hobby. I self-published a story about ten years ago. I like writing poetry as in a few words a lot can be said. It's a wonderful way of expressing what is going on in your thoughts. I enjoy travelling with my husband as we are both retired. We share 3 young grandchildren who also keep us active.

Denny Paul Mills: Forever a player in the english language .. bashed out-of-tune guitars since 1975 .. squashing prose into songs as a hobby as long as i remember .. it's not like i like poetry it slides off me like excess baggage .. and inspiration is all around .. we're blessed we're in a little world where things can be dug up n made alive again .. I'm in love with syllables

John Mcmahon: I'm John I'm 40 I live with my wife and daughter in sunny Dumbarton in Scotland I have been writing for 20 years I have won a couple of competitions. I have bipolar and because of this my writing is a (tad) dark. Please enjoys my work!

Ian OPG London: Poet, Songwriter and Bass Player in punk band No Feelings. Spends his time drinking JD and thinking too much.

Heather Snedden: I am 58years old and I live in the small town of Falkirk. Like a lot of people in the word today I have suffered mental health issues. I am not ashamed of this and I found my coping mechanism through the power of writing. I run a small writing group that is based around Mental Health and Wellbeing. We encourage & support one another.

Meek: Poet, singer, sinner, guitarist, subterranean, vegetarian almost vegan, writer, horticulturist, insomniac, procrastinator.

Wendy Webb: Born in the Midlands, Wendy found home and family life in Norfolk. She has edited Star Tips poetry magazine 2001-2021. Published in various small press magazines, winning a number of poetry competitions and self-publishing biography and poetry. Recently she has dabbled in local radio broadcasting and online poetry publications. She loves nature, the garden, the sea, photography and is always creative. Her two latest publications with Inherit the Earth:-

LANDSCAPES (joint poetry collection with David Norris-Kay & Wendy Webb)

Landscapes: Amazon.co.uk: Webb, Wendy Ann, Norris-Kay, David, Meek, CT, Meek, Norris-Kay, David: 9798851001659: Books

LOVE'S FLORELOQUENCE (Wendy Ann Webb)

Love's Floreloquence: Amazon.co.uk: Webb, Wendy Ann, Meek, CT, Meek: 9798850867003: Books

Susan Broadfoot: Been writing on and off for years. Written half a dozen short stories for children, one soon to be a musical. Took to songwriting in my fifties and living it. Prefer doing lyrics but I have a go at tunes. Dabbled in music theatre, folk music, classical singing. Sing in an Abba tribute band and as guest with several other bands. Got a few recording projects on the go. Recently collaborated on a project with Uri Geller.

David Norris-Kay: Well known in the small press as David Austin, David now writes under his Grandmother's and Mother's maiden names to commemorate their brothers who died in two world wars. He lives in Sheffield, England and his definitive poetry collection 'From Time-Buried Years' was published by

Indigo Dreams in 2009. Second edition with extra poems published in 2014. Now in its fourth reprint. David's poetry has won many awards and commendations.

Jon Bickley: Was born in London on 23rd October 1956. He is a poet, a folksinger and a songwriter. As a child he heard hymns in church, his mother singing Palgrave's Golden Treasury and the Beatles. Later it was Kerouac, Shakespeare and the Marx Brothers, now it is Yeats, Burnside and Heaney. Nothing much changes. He has self-published 3 volumes of poetry, released a dozen albums and is host of the Invisible Folk Club radio show and podcast.

Mark Ingram: Is committed to positive social change a supporter of CND and Green issues. A dedicated union officer protecting workers rights is a main driving force in his life. He lives in Lichfield with his partner Carol and Maxwell the cat and enjoys walking, reading and writing poetry and prose.

Des Lane: I was born in Fleetwood Lancashire but have lived in Wolverhampton for most of my life. I am married to Helen and we have 2 adult sons. I have a BA (Hons) degree in Fine Art and a Post Graduate Teaching Qualification and have actually made use of them both. I was Front of House Manager at Wolverhampton Art Gallery for 9 years and curated the country's first council funded Tattoo Art Exhibition which featured work by tattooist and friend Spike. I was also a founding member of the Community Arts Group: Arts Focus A.K.A Noisy Beasts which operated in the West Midlands and Staffordshire. I successfully applied for Arts Council Funding and Arts Focus was able to provide workshops and services to Wolverhampton Art Galleries, South Staffordshire Council, schools in both counties and The Custard Factory Birmingham. I am almost 60 and although I have played in bands, painted public murals, raised money for Birmingham Childrens Hospital and performed poetry live. I have literally been "Spending Too Much Time in the Thinking Shop" when it comes to getting published. To correct this I am currently working on my first poetry collection "Spending Too Much Time in the Thinking Shop" for Inherit The Earth Publishers.

George Colkitto: Winner of the Scottish Writers Poetry Competition 2012, Siar Sceal Hanna Greally Poetry Award 2014, Autumn Voices acrostic competition 2020, has poems in Linwood, Johnstone, and Erskine Health Centres. Recent publications are two poetry collections from Diehard Press and a pamphlet from Cinnamon Press.

Janette Fenton: was born in Glasgow, raised in The Highlands and lives in London. She is a semi-retired teacher, singer-songwriter, poet and environmentalist. Janette recently published her first volume of poems, Ripples and Waves of Life which is available on Amazon. She has also released 3 songs on YouTube and Spotify etc, Ghost of Life, That's How Close and Face Me. That's How Close has been played on American radio and on BBC Radio 5. It has also been entered for a Now That's What I call Lockdown compilation, which will go into the British Museum lockdown archives. Janette enjoys writing with others and has co-written the song So Easy by Steve Kopandy. She also runs the iconic music venue Facebook group, the Marquee Club, London.

Richard Earls: Performs poetry on the UK, New York and Paris spoken word circuit, and in a past life he was involved in the mid-80s UK jazz/pop scene. His two contributions were influenced by dreams. One, Barbie and Ken, a result of watching too much Fox News when he spent time in the States and the other, The Box and the Key, after finding an old portrait in the attic of a house he stayed in one Summer in France.

Steven Joseph McCrystal: Hi folks, I've been writing for several years now. Mainly as a hobby writer but I do have the writer's dream of writing a popular book. Over the years I've been published in a few places: Quailbell Magazine, The Scottish Book Trust, The Falkirk Herald newspaper, Asylum Magazine, and some of my art has been published in an online magazine called: Paper Dragon, a Drexel University publication, (Philadelphia). I should also include the various For the Many Not the Few publications that I've been part of. Especially my first book: Red Pill Memories. Plus, I have to include my Express Yourself on the radio antics. Express Yourself being the title of a Sunny Govan radio show for poets. I've sent in a few poems in to be aired and I sound terrible. I've also performed at various spoken word events within the Falkirk area. My attitude to creativity is the slow and steady approach mixed with outbursts of inspiration. I like to keep it fun with my poetry and writing. If I make someone smile, I'm happy too. Did I mention my abstract art? I've been plodding along with that for years too.

Giancarlo Moruzzi: My name is Giancarlo (known to my friends as John) Moruzzi, I was born in London to Italian immigrant Parents and we worked together in the catering trade. I have always had a passion for music and the blues I play guitar and I collect them. I started writing poetry in my teens and particularly like the classic poets and the beat poets. Some of my favourite poets include William Blake, Charles Baudelaire, Lawrence Ferlinghetti, Arthur Rimbaud and Rupert Brooke and obviously Bob Dylan. I think that passion for either music or art is a companion that remains with you the whole of your life.

Michelle Carr: I was born and still work and live in Glasgow. When I am not toiling at the office, I paint and write poetry. I love all things creative, from music to art, and I love collaborating with others to bring a creative project to fruition.

Naimh Mahon: Drama has always been at the heart of my life. As a trained actress, I've infused each role I've taken on, whether it's been as a Local Councillor, Teacher, Mother, Producer, Facilitator, or Storyteller, with passionate intensity. Born in Dublin, from a young age, I was immersed in theatre - studying and performing. Later, when I moved to London I enhanced my career in theatre, television, and film. I've embraced diverse roles and experiences. My career journey took an unexpected but successful turn into the world of technology, where I excelled with one of the leading computer giants of my time. Later, as head of a junior school, I approached teaching with the same ambition and achieved remarkable results. My Irish heritage has always influenced my analytical thinking and eloquent expression, setting me apart in every role. I find immense joy in engaging with fellow creatives, facilitating discussions, and sharing stories. In recent years, I've had the privilege of participating in prestigious events such as The Byline Festival and the Stafford Literary Festival as a storyteller. I've also played a pivotal role as Chair at the Rose Theatre in Rugeley, promoting productions like the Palmer Season of plays, where I took on a leading role. My life's journey embraces diverse passions and talents, thriving in the world of creativity, learning, and storytelling.

Lawrence Reed: After studying my masters in music composition I became interested in the rhythms and sounds of words. From there my poetry began. In 2020 a volume of my recent works entitled Earth's Secret Engine was published by Inherit The Earth Publication and is available on Amazon. I live in Bath and draw inspiration from the surrounding nature and the strange thoughts it inspires. I write music and lyrics for the prog-folk band Pagan Harvest and play guitar duets with Fight and Flight.
www.lawrencereed.com

Acknowledgements

Once again I am profoundly indebted to everyone who contributes to these volumes. None of this could happen without your input. Alone we'd be less strong.

Meek
October
2023

Inherit The Earth

inherit_theearth@btinternet.com

Other Volumes -

For The Many Not The Few Volume 1
ISBN: 9781719926010
For The Many Not The Few Volume 2
ISBN: 9781728809663
For The Many Not The Few Volume 3
ISBN: 9781730813436
For The Many Not The Few Volume 4
ISBN: 9781790289806
For The Many Not The Few Volume 5
ISBN: 9781793911438
For The Many Not The Few Volume 6
ISBN: 9781797777740
For The Many Not The Few Volume 7
ISBN: 9781092566001
For The Many Not The Few Volume 8
ISBN: 9781077465053
For The Many Not The Few Volume 9
ISBN: 9781688331341
For The Many Not The Few Volume 10
ISBN: 9781697057454
For The Many Not The Few Volume 11
ISBN: 9781709406850
For The Many Not The Few Volume 12
ISBN: 9781677498208
For The Many Not The Few Volume 13
ISBN: 9798618382052
For The Many Not The Few Volume 14
ISBN: 9798646549557
For The Many Not The Few Volume 15
ISBN: 9798664339031
For The Many Not The Few Volume 16
ISBN: 9798692012333
For The Many Not The Few Volume 17
ISBN: 9798700447607
For The Many Not The Few Volume 18
ISBN: 9798743558834
For The Many Not The Few Volume 19
ISBN: 9798532155923

For The Many Not The Few Volume 20
ISBN: 9798752349836
For The Many Not The Few Volume 21
ISBN: 9798779858649
For The Many Not The Few Volume 22
ISBN: 9798418065148
For The Many Not The Few Volume 23
ISBN: 9798808241787
For The Many Not The Few Volume 24
ISBN: 9798836629946
For The Many Not The Few Volume 25
ISBN: 9798849721484
For The Many Not The Few Volume 26
ISBN: 9798362428655
For The Many Not The Few Volume 27
ISBN: 9798371013743
For The Many Not The Few Volume 28
ISBN: 9798377782216
For The Many Not The Few Volume 29
ISBN: 9798392911639
For The Many Not The Few Volume 30
ISBN: 9798851393792
For The Many Not The Few Volume 31
ISBN: 9798860503533

All available from Amazon

Notes

Amazon KDP

Printed in Great Britain
by Amazon